Forever a

Publicist Olivia Sinclair has been away from Windswept Bay for years busy helping the Hollywood elite get out of one scandal after another. But now, she's in the middle of a scandal herself, involving a big name actor and suddenly, coming home to lay low in Windswept Bay is her own best advice to herself.

Life has just gotten complicated for charter boat captain, Brandon "BJ" McCall. He's recently learned he has a brother and he's inherited half of a multi-million dollar corporation that could alter life as he knows it. Finding a beautiful, shorty pajama clad female, frozen in fear on the roof of her house is a complication he doesn't mind at all.

Terrified and stuck on her roof…and in only her pj's and being rescued by a stranger who could rival any of her Hollywood clients isn't exactly what Olivia had planned. She's trying to get off the cover of the gossip magazines—not hold her spot for eternity! Falling into the arms of a stranger, who turns out to be the long lost brother of her sister's husband—and is a walking news worthy scandal in his own right, is not a smart PR move.

Not to mention the family complications it could make if things didn't work out between them. Plus, she has plans to go back to Hollywood the minute she thinks the smoke has cleared.

It's all just too complicated.

But, on the beaches of Windswept Bay romance is in the air and love is a complication that just might be undeniable.

FOREVER AND FOR ALWAYS

Windswept Bay, Book Four

DEBRA CLOPTON

Forever and For Always

Copyright © 2016 Debra Clopton Parks

CHAPTER ONE

Olivia Sinclair rolled over in bed and tugged the pillow over her head as the cat wailed just outside her window. "Go away," she groaned. She needed sleep. Just a little sleep was all she was asking for.

The wail came again.

"Give me a break, kitty," she groaned. "Go away."

She'd left Hollywood hours before dawn two days ago and driven the two thousand, three hundred miles to Windswept Bay. She'd tried to sleep for short periods in a couple of small-town hotels, one in the

Texas Panhandle and one in Mississippi, but she hadn't been able to get much sleep while her mind was overtaxed with the scandal that was going on in her life.

She'd had to wear a baseball cap and sunshades every time she stopped for gas. And when she went inside a store for a cup of coffee or a soda, she'd had to keep her head down and hope no one standing in line with her happened to look at the cover photos on the magazine racks beside the counter...her picture was plastered over several of the tabloids. Of course, in most of them, her face was partly hidden by mega movie star Brad Pearson's face as he startled her with a kiss that came out of nowhere.

What had he been thinking? What had he been doing?

She was still reeling from it and the complications his odd action had produced in her life. The scandal his kiss had started threatened to end her career. He was her client at the public relations firm she worked for and until that moment, their relationship had strictly business, as required by her firm. And her own moral code where clients were concerned.

She didn't want to think about that right now.

She wanted to sleep.

Something she hadn't had for days as she had been trying to stop the runaway media blitz the kiss had started.

The worst of it was that she should have seen it coming. Should have seen some sign that his feelings for her had shifted...but she hadn't.

The wail came again. *Maybe something was wrong with the cat...* She groaned and pulled the pillow from her head; she couldn't ignore a cat in trouble. She sat up. "Okay, okay."

She glanced at the clock and felt like crying. It was only five thirty. Blurry-eyed and feeling as if she were moving through a tunnel of sleep deprivation, she padded barefoot through the house and out onto the deck, only to realize it was a misty morning.

The mist had rolled in since she'd arrived a whole three hours ago. She glanced down the short path and out across the very wide expanse of white sand that separated the bungalow from the water. The mist was probably going to turn into rain by the looks of the stormy early morning sky.

The wail came again and she spun to glance toward the sound. A small yellow cat sat on the edge of the roof.

"How did you get up there?" Olivia glanced around for a limb of some kind that the cat might have used. She saw one; she could see how the cat could have dropped from the branch of the ten-foot-tall palm near the end of the house or maybe it climbed up the firebush shrub and dove for the roof. Either one would clearly cause a problem getting back down. With a moan, Olivia bit her bottom lip and rubbed her forehead as the thought of climbing up a ladder to rescue the cat sank in. Her chest tightened at the very idea. Heights were not her strong point. Frankly, they were her Achilles' heel, terrifying her in a really petrifying way.

The cat wailed again and tilted its head to look down at her. It looked pitiful.

"Oh, this is so not good." But clearly, getting the cat down was the only way to get back to sleep. *She could do this.* She could get the ladder, climb to the roof edge, and scoop the cat up and rescue it, and then she'd climb right back down. No looking down, no looking around. She'd be okay.

She hurried from the deck to the small shed hidden in the trees for the groundskeeper of the larger estate that this bungalow sat on. Her sister had a really sweet deal going that enabled her to live in the bungalow and house-watch the place during the year for the seasonal owners. They rarely visited, as was the same for most of the other homeowners on the exclusive, private beach.

When she opened the door, Olivia spotted the ladder leaning against the wall; she pulled it out and then dragged it across the sand. She carried it up onto the deck and propped it against the roof and then checked it for sturdiness. Her mouth was dry and her palms damp—she could blame it on the mist but she knew it was perspiration. Sweaty palms were not becoming but when it came to heights, she had them.

Her stomach churned as she placed her foot on the rung and realized that she wore her shorty pajamas.

She paused. *Maybe she should change.* The wail of the cat nixed that idea. Besides, there was no one around and she would only be using it as an excuse to put off what she must do. Her churning stomach turned into rough seas as she forced one foot at a time onto a new, higher rung. The mist caused the metal to feel slick, which only added to her anxiety. With her eyes barely squinting—this was to prevent peripheral sight—she reached the roof edge.

The cat, however, had retreated farther down the roofline.

Olivia tried to call out to the cat but only squeaked instead. She cleared her throat and tried again and this time actual words came out. "Here kitty, kitty."

The cat wailed.

Olivia felt the dread of moving up onto the roof all the way through her like a case of the flu gone bad, bad, bad. Her heart palpitations were erratic as she moved her hands to the top of the ladder. Gritting her teeth, she moved up a rung and then placed her hands on the roof and her fingers felt sick...like weak knees.

Ever since she was a child, she'd had this

"problem."

"Focus on the helpless cat," she muttered and squinted at the roofline through one eye. "Do not look down." She enunciated each word like a decree and slowly crawled from the ladder to the wet shingles. She slipped and her foot pushed against the ladder rung as she frantically grappled for something to hang onto. Thankfully, she didn't slip down the roof.

But the ladder crashed to the deck, making her jump.

And making the cat run. It dove to the palm branch and disappeared from sight.

Olivia gaped, mouth open at the spot where it disappeared. "Ahh, why you," she said shakily just as the mist turned to a drizzle. And her weary spirits plummeted.

"Thanks a lot," she muttered darkly and shot a glance heavenward. "It's been a great week."

Focusing on not looking down and not slipping, she managed to move from her knees to her rump. The rough grate of the shingles did not feel good through the thin material of her PJs. Eyeing the satellite dish sitting just out of reach, but too shaken to move, she pulled her knees up and clasped her arms around them. Trying not to hyperventilate and starting to wail herself, she rested her chin on her knees and focused on the water in the distance. If she stared at the water, she could pretend she was nine feet down on the deck.

All she had to do was not look down and she'd be okay.

The problem was, how would she get off the roof?

BJ McCall wasn't sure what was more unexpected as he halted his jog on the rain-drenched private beach and stared at the small bungalow across the sand: was it the thoroughly soaked female perched on the roof, or that she had pink flamingos plastered all over the scrap of soggy wet material that she wore?

What was she doing up there?

It had been a long week and he'd had several consecutive sleepless nights adjusting to the fact that almost everything he'd believed about his life had been a lie. This news he'd just learned this past week had him still reeling and trying to come to grips with it. But he wasn't sure that was possible. Thus, his early morning jog on the misty beach...the private beach where his new brother's home was located. The home he'd just learned was half his.

Being a man who had never wanted a home or believed in being tied down, he lived on his boat and went where the wind or his notions carried him. The news he was processing was both disturbing and disrupting to his world as he knew it. Or wanted it.

The woman on the roof wasn't moving.

Was she real? Or maybe a figment of his sleep-deprived mind?

He rubbed his eyes, almost believing the woman perched on the roof like a weather vane in the middle of the rainy morning really could be a figment of his weary and overtaxed brain.

But when he squinted through the increasing haze of raindrops, she was still there.

Yep, she was as real as could be.

9

Learning that he had an older brother and a father he'd never known who had died recently and left him, not only an older brother and half of a huge home on a private beach in picturesque Windswept Bay, but also half ownership of a multi-million dollar company based in New York—*Manhattan*, New York—was a shock.

Manhattan. One place that, despite his wanderlust, had never appealed to him.

He wanted open space and the thought of all those buildings and sky only visible if you looked straight up was not on his bucket list.

And dollars… He was a simple man and had what he needed.

Need. This woman obviously needed help.

He moved forward and saw her tugging on the short gown, or maybe it was the top of a set of short pajamas. If she didn't look so miserable he might have smiled, but he felt bad for her and so there was no smile.

He strode toward the short trail to the house just as

the drizzle suddenly turned into a downpour. And still she made no move to get off the roof. BJ frowned and started to jog. Something about this picture was definitely not right.

CHAPTER TWO

"This is not funny anymore," Olivia muttered as the deluge rained down upon her. She shot a furious glare heavenward through strands of soaked hair as the pouring rain drenched her.

Terror of slipping off the wet roof and plunging to the rough deck paralyzed her more, but she managed to shift slowly until she had locked her hands onto the small satellite dish. It was cold and slick from the rain but gave her something more than her knees to hold onto as the rain beat down on her. Her hair hung like a wet cloak over her face; she wanted so badly to shove it out of her eyes but she didn't dare let go of the metal disk she clung to.

She was too close to the edge—just thinking about it had her feeling ill and wanting to claw handfuls of roof shingles in an attempt to feel less vulnerable. She closed her eyes against the rain rolling over her and she concentrated on not moving. Her feet felt as if they were on slick ice with the rain now running downhill from the rooftop and cascading over the edge in a waterfall. Which gave her visions of being swept over in the deluge.

"Are you in trouble?"

Startled by the deep voice, she glanced down briefly to see the hooded man she'd seen out on the beach as she'd been staring at the ocean moments ago. He stared up at her from the deck. Her stomach tilted from looking down and she quickly focused back on the beach.

She'd seen him pause on the beach, but she'd been too embarrassed to wave a hand for help like a normal person would have done. Instead, she'd been weighing the consequences of her actions, torn between calling out for help or wishing he would go away—she was, after all, wearing these silly Florida flamingo shorty PJs.

And then there was the other reason. She was already in enough hot water with the tabloids. It would be just the kind of luck she'd been having for this guy to snap a photo and later realize that he could make a mint selling her out to a tabloid. Or, for all she knew, he could be the first of the paparazzi who had located her and he was about to get the scoop of his life.

And she really wasn't even the scoop. Any female would have been in her spot if they'd been photographed with mega movie star Brad Pearson laying a hot, passionate kiss on her! The very memory sent heated indignation racing through Olivia. Brad had totally and completely blindsided her with that kiss. And now the photographers had labeled her the mystery woman and were in hot pursuit of a story.

Her photo was on every magazine rack in every grocery and convenience store across the country. *Mystery woman—ha!* She wished. The only mystery to her was what her client had been thinking.

And what had she been thinking when she'd crawled up this ladder in her pajamas, of all things?

Olivia glanced quickly back at the hooded man standing in the downpour and staring up at her. *What was he doing walking on a beach in the rain?*

And he's probably wondering who would be on a slick rooftop in the rain.

She had made bad judgment calls lately. Climbing up on the roof to rescue the crying cat had not been one of her smartest moves considering she was terrified of heights.

But then, it could be for lack of sleep that she'd made this one. Lack of sleep and empathy for the cat. Maybe it was scared of heights too... *Okay, dumb but well, she was tired.*

And here she was on the wet, slick roof with her toes tingling, her heart thundering erratically, and a very real need to toss her cookies—if she'd eaten any cookies that morning.

That darn cat, the little darling, better run when— or *if*—she ever got down from this rooftop.

"Are you all right?" he asked from way down

below and drew her back from her meltdown.

Her eyes narrowed and she was glad her hair was somewhat acting as a disguise. "I'm on a roof in the drizzling rain. In pink flamingo shorty PJs—" Olivia gasped, as dawning hit her of how exposed she was in this outfit. She crossed her arms over her boobage— gifts from Aunt Marge that Olivia would readily disinherit if only it were possible. She could probably win a wet T-shirt contest right now. Though, hopefully, pink flamingos didn't show off as much as white T-shirts. Her arms crossed, she awkwardly clung to the satellite dish, feeling as if she were playing a game of Twister.

"Did your ladder fall?"

She glared at him and slipped, very ungracefully. "No," she snapped. "I kicked it down on purpose." *Who was this guy?*

And why are you being a shrew when you need his help?

She shot a peek at him and he had a cross between pity and worry on his face.

"Sorry, I'm fine," she quipped, and tried for

nonchalance. But her hands slipped and she wobbled again. The roof was getting slicker.

"Steady," he urged. "I get it. You're afraid of heights."

"Bingo," she squeaked. *Don't look down. Don't look down. Don't throw up. Don't throw up.*

"What are you doing on a roof if you're scared of heights?"

Her fingers dug into the metal. "I was *trying* to save a cat," she gritted through clenched teeth. "But the ungrateful feline saved herself." She ventured a glance down and saw the man had flung off his hood and she realized he was a very hunky man. She also saw his lips twitch.

She yanked her gaze away and tried not to think diabolical thoughts about his demise. After all, he was her only salvation at the moment.

"So you decided to just stay up there? After she saved herself?"

Kill. "No, are you kidding?" she snapped. "I want down. Should have never gotten up here in the first place. But with the drizzle making my ladder slippery,

I accidently kicked it down as I was getting on the roof. And now I'm stuck. And it's pouring."

"I see that," he called.

Did she hear laughter in his voice? There was a scraping noise and she opened eyes that she hadn't even realized she'd closed. The ladder was beside her. And then he was at eye level with her and yes, he was one hunky man. With the bluest eyes…and he was about to save her. She literally could kiss him right then and there. If she could pry her fingers from the satellite dish.

"May I help you off this roof?" He smiled and her nauseous stomach rippled with butterflies.

Ha. She didn't do butterflies. No, in her business, amazingly good-looking and charismatic men were the norm. And not to be toyed with. Case in point—tabloid fodder would follow.

He held out his hand to her and smiled an amazing smile, so amazing that the heavens saw fit to stop raining cats and dogs in that moment.

"That would be nice," she managed but couldn't force her fingers to let go of the satellite dish and take his hand.

BJ tried to ignore the jolt of attraction that he felt the moment her green eyes met his through her mass of wet blonde hair. She was scared but trying hard not to fall apart. He felt for her. He'd once had an accident and gotten trapped inside a small dark shed. He could still remember the panic he'd felt until his father had found him an hour later and rescued him. *His father. The father who'd raised him…* He pushed the confusing thoughts away and focused on the beauty staring at him.

Her blonde hair was plastered to her head, but it just accentuated her oval face and big eyes. Something was familiar about her. "Do I know you?" He didn't think he would have ever forgotten her if he'd ever met her, but there was something about her.

She paled, if that was possible because she was already pale from fright. "No, I'm pretty sure we haven't met." She looked down, letting her wet hair cover her face more.

"No, I'm pretty sure we've met."

"We haven't."

"I don't forget faces. At least not like yours."

Her expression, or what he could see through all that hair, tensed.

"I just got to town." She sounded emphatic and a little agitated.

"Okay," he said slowly and let it go because the last thing he needed was for her to freeze up more than she already was. She was obviously petrified. "So let me get this straight. You are deathly afraid of heights, but to save your cat, you climbed up here anyway and managed to kick the ladder down and strand yourself."

"It's not my cat and I wouldn't say I was deathly afraid, exactly."

He squinted. "You sure about that?"

She sighed. "It's true but I don't like to accept it." She glanced up at him and those green eyes got him right in the gut.

"I guess you could look on the bright side. You climbed up here to be a hero. Sounds like you might have made some progress by getting up here in the first place."

"True. But if you hadn't come along, I guess I'd be up here until someone missed me and came searching. And since no one knows I'm here..." The last words were more of a mutter.

"I've got it," he said, as suddenly he knew. "You're Shar's sister. We met at the hospital when Gage was in the hospital."

She held her head up then and looked him straight in the eye; he could have sworn he saw relief in her eyes.

"Oh, you've met my sisters, Jillian and Shar." She gave a small laugh and yes, it was a relieved laugh. "We're triplets. Though Shar isn't identical, Jillian and I are...at least to those who don't know us well."

"So that explains it. I knew that I knew you and wondered why you were hiding it. I was starting to think you had something to hide," he teased.

"Um, no...I just haven't met you. So, you were at the hospital?"

"Yeah. I'm BJ McCall."

It took a moment for his name to register. And

then dawning showed in those eyes.

"You're Gage's brother. The one he just found."

"Yeah, it was a very unusual day." *That was the understatement of the century.*

"I'm sure it was," she said, softly.

They stared at each other and the moment stretched between them. He knew that she and Jillian might be identical, and when she had dry hair and was less pale, he was sure now they'd look exactly alike except the buzz of attraction he felt had not happened between him and Jillian. Her green eyes had not reached inside him like these were doing right now.

"You're Olivia, right?" He was pretty sure he'd remembered someone saying her name.

"Yes, that's me."

"Well, Olivia, are you ready to get down now?"

"Again, yes, I am. That is the best idea I've heard in days. If I can let go of this satellite dish."

He smiled and reached across her to take one of her hands in his. He squeezed her hand gently. "You can do it. Move this way a little and let's get you on this ladder."

She took a deep breath and held his gaze as she inched to the ladder. She was still holding tight to the satellite dish with her other hand and he realized that looking down wasn't exactly where he needed to be looking. Her clingy, wet pajamas left little to the imagination and though he found himself tempted…he held her gaze instead.

"You have to let go of that." He nodded to her other hand.

"Oh," she gasped and instantly yanked her hand from the satellite dish to grasp the ladder.

"There you go. Now take a deep breath and put your foot on the rung."

It took a little while but they managed to make it to the ground at last. Once there, she spun around and flung her arms around his neck.

"Thank you," she gasped. Then yanked herself back a foot, as if startled by her actions, and crossed her arms securely over her breasts. "Sorry, I don't normally throw my arms around men, but I can't thank you enough. And now, I need to go change. Wait, though. Please." She turned, opened the glass door and stepped inside.

He was left standing in the drizzle, thinking about those blasted pink flamingos—among other things.

She returned in a moment with a warmup top and pants. "Sorry. I doubt I'll ever wear those pajamas again in my life." She laughed a lovely embarrassed laugh.

He grinned. "That's a pity."

She laughed again. "Maybe from where you were standing. But believe me, they will not bring back good memories for me. Would you like to come in for some coffee to warm up? I can give you a towel."

"No, that's okay. My boat is down there at the dock." He waved a hand toward where his charter boat was tied to the private dock. "I'm staying at the house while Gage and Shar are on their honeymoon. It's down the beach there."

She smiled. "And I'm staying a few days here at Shar's. I'm…" She looked thoughtful for a moment. "Housesitting for her."

"I guess I'm doing that too, in a way." Gage had given him the key to the house that they owned. The house that contained more of the photos of him as a child with his mother and Milton Lancaster. Gage had said that he was welcome to stay there and to go through the photos and anything else he found. As it turned out, they were both seeking answers. Gage just had the priority of getting married to take precedence over learning more about their complicated pasts.

As much as BJ hadn't wanted to accept the offer, he'd been compelled to come over yesterday and go through the photos. And then he'd spent the night there.

He wasn't sure how long he was going to stay.

As he looked into her soft green eyes, he was tempted to take that cup of coffee. "Stay safe." He turned and walked away. He had a lot on his mind right now. The best thing he could do was to not let himself get lost in those green eyes.

Olivia watched BJ walk away and she ignored the pull of attraction. The last thing she needed right now was *that*.

She was just relieved that he'd been a normal man who'd obviously paid no attention to the magazine racks. That fact alone made him attractive to her. And the fact that he'd saved her from her ridiculous situation and not ridiculed her for her fear meant he was a simply a nice guy.

Heaving in a sigh, she headed into the kitchen and made herself a cup of coffee.

With coffee in hand, she went back to the bedroom and sat cross-legged in the warm covers of her bed while she sipped the coffee.

Against her better judgment, she decided to check her messages.

There were four voice messages from Brad—begging her to call him, because he had to see her.

The man had lost it. Obviously. She set her coffee on the table along with the phone that she'd set on silence a long time ago. And then she snuggled under the covers and closed her eyes.

She would handle this tomorrow. Right now, she wanted to play like an ostrich and ignore the trouble and try to get some sleep.

Maybe then she'd be fortified enough to deal with this.

The only problem was that when she closed her eyes, BJ McCall was smiling at her with those teal-blue eyes that made her think of tropical days on the beach and moonlit kisses...

CHAPTER THREE

The day after her rooftop fiasco, a little more rested and feeling better, Olivia parked Olivia's jeep in the back of the parking lot, having decided it might be better to keep her car parked just in case a reporter might just happen to be around and have her license plate number. She told herself she was being paranoid but left the car in the garage anyway. She used the rear entrance to enter the Windswept Bay Resort. Her parents had owned the beautiful boutique resort since before her birth and now her three sisters were running it. When they'd banded together to take over the running of the resort when their parents had decided to retire, Olivia had opted not to go in with her sisters. Not that she didn't want the legacy of the resort to go on, but because her life was in Hollywood. She was building her career and hadn't planned to ever live back on the picturesque island again. She loved her life. She did.

This was just a setback.

Tugging the wide brim of her hat forward on her forehead, she strode through the elegantly landscaped grounds that her talented sister, Jillian, designed. When she spotted a female bottom sticking out of a shrub, she paused.

"Please tell me you haven't fallen into a gopher hole."

"What?" Jillian gasped, spinning in the dirt to gape up at her. "Olivia!" She laughed and scrambled from the dirt, brushing at her knees before she wrapped her arms around Olivia. "What are you doing here? We've been so worried about you."

Olivia laughed and hugged her look-alike back. "I've been on the road. Keeping to myself and heading this way. I had to get out of town for a few days and I just took off."

Jillian leaned back from her and studied her with serious intent. "You look worn out."

"Gee, thanks. I got to Shar's night before last and spent much of yesterday catching up on my sleep."

"And you didn't let us know?"

Olivia shook her head. "I was too tired." She decided to omit her rooftop adventure, at least for now. "And I needed time to get my thoughts together."

"Well, come on. We need to get you out of sight." Jillian tucked her arm in hers and they started toward the back of the garden. The path led to the back entrance of the offices.

Her sisters had seen her photo on the cover of the tabloid last week and called her, so they knew she'd gotten herself into a bind. But she hadn't really explained anything to them. She'd been in her I-can-handle-it mode of operation. And well, she hadn't been able to. The kissing picture and more murky shots the tabloids claimed were her as the "mystery woman" had emerged. These photos were not her but there was no

30

convincing anyone of the truth. So here she was. Home with her tail tucked between her legs.

"Thanks, sis."

"Anytime. Cali and I and all the brothers, along with Mom and Dad, have been very worried about you. But we were giving you space. After all, we didn't know if you and Brad were going to show up and tell us you were getting married—like the tabs claim. Or maybe you would tell us you two lovebirds had already gotten married."

Olivia came to an abrupt halt. "You did not believe that? Tell me that you did not believe that."

Jillian smiled sweetly; she was the sweetest of all the sisters. "No, of course not. I'm just teasing. Ease up. But you have to admit that was one whopping kiss you two were sharing in those photos. I mean goodness, it's a wonder you didn't catch on fire or something."

Olivia couldn't help laughing at that. "Well, a photo is not always truthful." *Boy, was that the truth.*

She tugged open the door and Jillian led the way up the stairs. "Cali is going to be so excited. We are so glad you're here. It's been too long, Olivia."

"I know."

A few minutes later, Cali jumped up from her desk and rushed Olivia like a kid after an ice cream cone. "Olivia!" She swept her into a hug.

As the older sister, Cali had always been there for the triplets. Now she immediately began giving Olivia the third degree that Jillian had already started.

"Why didn't you call? Why didn't you let us know where you were? Come, sit, and tell us everything." As she drilled Olivia, Jillian closed the office door so they had privacy. "Why was Brad Pearson kissing you?" Cali finally asked as they all sat down in the seating area in the corner.

Olivia frowned. "That is a great question. I have no idea."

"Have you and him been dating?" Cali asked.

"No. He is my client. I have had to get that man out of more touchy situations with the media than I can even count without my laptop. The man sleeps with countless women. Married or not, as has been well publicized in the media and the tabloids."

Jillian rubbed her temple. "So why? What's brought this on?"

Once again, she was baffled. "I truly don't know. I am completely professional when I am around him. I'm not even attracted to him."

"Not at all?" Jillian asked in disbelief.

Cali held up a hand with her fingers pinched together. "Not even a tiny bit?"

"No, he's disgusting. And so was that kiss. I mean yes, he knows how to kiss, but girls, he just grabbed me out of the blue and plastered that thing on me like pancake mix on a cold skillet."

Both her sisters burst into laughter.

"Oh, Olivia, you do have a way with words."

"That is so true." Cali chuckled. "Maybe it's your humor that got to him."

"I'm always serious when I'm with a client. The tabs will eat you alive if you're not. And the papa-*rats*-ies"—she emphasized *rat*—"as you can see, will believe or make believe anything they see."

"Did you try talking to them after he kissed you?"

"I didn't have time. Brad started laughing happily

33

and pulled me inside the waiting car. Once I was inside, I was just ready to get away from the cameras. I try really hard to always stay out of the cameras. I'm a voice of reason for my clients. I help them make statements more becoming or to get out of situations. I'm not supposed to be in the limelight. Nor do I want to be in it. And now, this."

"But you're good with words. You can tell the truth. Tell them it was nothing." Jillian's words and expression were in earnest.

"They want a story. And I haven't looked at Twitter or anything but I'm sure by now they know who I am. So if it's not on there now, by tomorrow not only my face but my name will be everywhere."

"Well, that just stinks," Cali snapped. "But it doesn't matter. We can handle this."

That was just it. Olivia wasn't sure they could.

"I need to go see Levi." Her big brother was the chief of police in Windswept Bay and he needed to know that trouble would likely be showing up today or tomorrow. Unless something huge happened in Hollywood that would take the focus off her. Other than that, the town was about to be full of hedge-hiding, camera-lugging photographers looking to score big any way they could.

She wasn't sure suddenly whether coming home had been the right thing to do.

"Come on." Cali stood. "Let's get out of here and go see Levi."

Jillian jumped up too. "Let's do it. We need to warn him before it gets wild. You know how he doesn't like being uninformed."

Olivia's heart swelled as she stared up at her sisters. It felt good to be home. To feel their support. She rose and put her arms around each of them and hugged them. "It's good to be home. I've been gone too long."

"Yes, you have," Cali said, gently. "But you have a life away from here and you always know you can come home when you want to for as long or as short a time as you want."

Olivia smiled. "So true. But, on the other hand, I feel like I've cut and run. And it doesn't feel right to me."

Jillian glared at her. "You are just gathering the wagons, as they say in the West. Nothing wrong with stepping back and assessing the situation. Besides, Hunky Pearson started this. Just tell them the man loves you and you don't reciprocate. That'll really stir the pot."

Olivia laughed. "I might decide to do that. But first, let's go talk to Chief Levi."

The rain had given way to a blue sky as BJ entered the Windswept Bay Police Station. Levi Sinclair was the police chief and BJ met him after a thug had tried to hijack his boat. Gage had come to reveal to BJ that they were brothers and had interrupted the hijacking and gotten shot trying to help BJ. Only after Levi arrived and they'd all ended up at the hospital while Gage was in surgery did he realize that Gage had stopped by his boat on the way to his wedding. Shar and the wedding party and family had all been at the hospital and it still seemed surreal to BJ, walking into that with Levi beside him. He hadn't learned until days later, when Gage was being released, that he was Gage's brother. BJ's life as he'd believed it to be since he was born had changed that day when Gage told him they were brothers. And told him that his mother had taken BJ as a baby and run away, hiding him from Gage's dad. His dad.

Levi was someone he felt he could become friends with and right now he needed a friend. He looked up from his computer when BJ entered.

"BJ, it's about time you came around. We were sorry you didn't show up at the wedding."

He hadn't been ready to accept all the life-changing information at the time of the wedding and so he'd not attended. "I had a lot to deal with. But Gage and Shar stopped by before they left for the airport and we talked. I'm happy for them, but I wasn't exactly ready to embrace my new past with my life as I've always known it. I'm still struggling, actually."

Levi's forehead creased and he looked sympathetic to BJ's situation. "I can understand it. I like my past. My family, my history. I don't think I'd be thrilled if someone walked through that door and told me it wasn't what it seemed."

"It's a lot to take in. But I'm trying to be open-minded. Gage insisted on giving me a key to the house that we are supposed to now own together. He wanted me to spend time there and go through the things they found that might help me learn more about my younger years. My past."

"So how's that going?"

BJ shrugged. "I stayed at the house the last couple of nights. I'm looking through all these photos of me and this man I do not remember. And then the pictures of me and my mom and him together…she just looked so young and happy. I just don't get why she left if she was that happy. But anyway, I came by to see if you were free for lunch. I'm new in town, sick of thinking about all of this, and I figure I owe you a meal for showing up and saving the day."

Levi stood. "I don't turn down free meals." He strode around his desk. "Let me tell the dispatcher where to find me then we'll head out."

They left his office and he went through another door; BJ heard him telling the woman behind the desk what he was doing.

The door from the street opened and to BJ's surprise, Olivia, Jillian—her look-alike—and Cali, the older sister, walked inside. When Olivia saw him, she came to an abrupt halt but Cali came straight to him and hugged him.

"BJ, it's great to see you. We missed you at the wedding. Please tell me you haven't had another morning of disaster on that boat of yours?"

He laughed. "Hey Cali, it's good to see you. Sorry about the wedding and no, I haven't had trouble on my boat. I just had a lot on my mind." He glanced back at Olivia and started to speak but Jillian beat him to it.

"I can't understand how overwhelmed you must have been. Probably still are. But anyway, this is our sister Olivia. She surprised us with a visit." She had grabbed Olivia's arm and tugged her to stand beside her.

"We've met, actually." It was obvious that she hadn't told them that they'd met or Jillian wouldn't have introduced him. So it didn't take a scientist to realize she probably hadn't told them she'd been stuck on her roof.

"Yes, we met on the beach this morning. BJ stayed at Gage's place last night."

Cali looked from him to Olivia. "You didn't mention it, Olivia."

"I didn't have time. We had a lot to talk about."

"True, we did," Jillian agreed.

Olivia smiled at him. "It's good to see you again."

"So you stayed at the house," Cali said. "Did you go through some of the photos that Shar told us about?"

"I did."

Levi came into the room. "Hey, Olivia. What are you doing here?"

"I came to give my big brother a hug."

"Well, if that's what got you home, then I'm glad you came."

BJ watched as Levi swept his sister up in a big hug. He also watched how her expression turned joyous as she hugged him.

"It's good to have you home," Levi said after a moment.

BJ suddenly felt out of place. "Hey, Levi, you're probably about to get a lunch invitation from these lovely ladies, so why don't we do lunch tomorrow?"

"Oh, we wouldn't want to stop you two from going to lunch," Olivia said.

"But we do need a quick moment with Levi," Jillian added.

"How about we all go?" Levi offered.

BJ shook his head. "No, maybe another time. Today you go. From what I understand, you haven't seen Olivia in a while. We'll do this later. Ladies, have a nice day. It was good to see you."

"Please come by and see us," Jillian said. "You're part of our family now and we'd love to get to know you better." She smiled genuinely.

"Thanks. I'll do that."

Olivia studied him. "You really are welcome to join us. I hate to steal Levi away from you."

He laughed. "It's not a problem. I'll talk to you later, Levi." A few minutes later, he was walking back down the street, thinking about Olivia. Something about her got him in his gut. Her sisters looked so very much like her and yet when those eyes of hers hit his, there was no denying that there was something different in her effect on him. And he had noticed instantly that there was a difference in her and her identical sister. Something in the way she carried herself, and the turn of her head as she spoke or even listened. He'd be able to pick out Olivia from Jillian just at a glance. Despite everything going on in his life right now, he wanted to find out more about Olivia.

He stopped at a convenience store to grab a pack of gum and a bottle of water and stood in line behind a couple of young girls. They were chattering away as they waited for the guy in front of them to get checked out.

"Oh look," one gasped and grabbed a magazine off the rack. "He is so sexy. And I loved his last movie."

BJ nearly rolled his eyes at this young girl gushing over some movie star.

The other one sighed. "He's a hunk. I'd kiss him any day. Can you believe they still don't know who the mystery girlfriend is?"

"I know. I heard online that they think it could be his publicity manager or something."

Bored but curious about who the mystery woman was, BJ glanced at the magazine they'd been ogling and saw the action flick movie star kissing some new blonde girlfriend. He was completely not interested in the dude's love life. He was about to look away when something about the blonde woman pretty much being swallowed whole by the guy on the cover grabbed his attention. He leaned closer. *No way.* His heart thumped double time as he reached out and snagged a copy for himself. The girls were walking out as he slapped the gossip magazine on the counter. He had to control his urge to stop the flow of the line as he studied the shot. He pulled dollars from his pocket and then tucked the magazine under his arm and headed out of the store. Once he made it outside on the sidewalk, he strode toward the marina and his boat.

As he walked, he stared down at the photo. And there on the side of the page was a clear photo of Olivia. Olivia and the "hunk" Brad Pearson.

He halted and couldn't help it as he thumbed to

the article page and read the latest news on the mystery girlfriend.

It didn't fit. But then, he didn't know Olivia. Not really. All he knew was that she was scared of heights and she'd shown up in town unannounced.

She was hiding out. The heat of publicity surrounding her and her boyfriend's ousted relationship must have driven her to lay low for a few days.

BJ tore his eyes off the article and then folded the magazine and tucked it under his arm as he strode the last block to the dock.

He was still in shock as he released the lines and headed back out for the day.

What was she thinking? You'd have to live off the grid completely not to have heard some of the stories of this guy's love life. He was in the news all the time.

And Olivia Sinclair was his latest squeeze.

CHAPTER FOUR

"So let me get this straight: you think those crazy paparazzi are coming to my town again? Hunting you?" Levi's expression was stern and one of disbelief. "Olivia, I thought you were smarter than this?"

"I am. I did not kiss him. He blindsided me."

"How?" Levi's gaze narrowed.

Olivia's stomach churned. "I am not naïve. There were no warning signs that he was even attracted to me. It came out of nowhere when he grabbed me in front of the paparazzi and kissed me. It was almost like it was planned."

"That creep." He gave her a hug. "I hope he comes to town."

Olivia loved her brothers. They were all supportive and would stand by her no matter what. "Thank you." She hugged him back.

"That said, we better get ready because the press hounds will be coming. You're absolutely right. Man, I hate the bush hogs."

Cali laughed. "I think Grant ruined Levi on the paparazzi. When they came to town in helicopters and vans, poor Levi and his deputies had to control the chaos."

"It was the danger that they put everyone in. And people should have a right to their privacy, even if they are a celebrity."

"Exactly," Olivia said. "But as much as the celebrities hate it, they need them. Brad Pearson would dry up and wither if the paparazzi weren't following him around, keeping him in the news. His love life is the new biggest thing since Brangelina."

"Branja-who?" Levi scowled.

All three of his sisters laughed.

Olivia placed a hand on his arm. "Brad Pitt and Angelina Jolie. The celebrity power couple. The paparazzi put their names together to represent their relationship. And now the same tabloids are going crazy because they're splitting up and Brangelina is no more."

"I still don't get it," Levi muttered, his brows drawn together.

"Of course you don't and thankfully so." Cali laughed. "They put the first few letters of his name then added *n* and then added the last letters of her name. Brangelina."

"That's crazy." Levi looked unimpressed.

"So true," Jillian agreed.

"As much as I may hate it too, things like that are what my job thrives on. Public relations advisors need controversy to keep their jobs going. Getting the celeb out of a fix is what keeps me working."

"And you like it?" Levi asked skeptically.

She hitched a shoulder. "Sometimes. But it does get old." She didn't want to add that she was beginning get disillusioned. This hadn't been her first choice for a career but she was very good at what she did. Having been recruited by the best company in the business spoke to her ability. This incident wasn't going to help her situation at all.

Later, as she left her family and headed back home, she longed for the convertible that she once had. Her thoughts drifted to BJ as she headed toward her sister's house. *Would he be near? Had he seen a tabloid yet?*

And if he had seen one, what would be his reaction?

Her job required her to go through all aspects of a situation, analyze it and come up with the best solution to solve it.

She hoped he hadn't seen the photos. Wished they didn't exist and that he was just a guy she'd met under normal circumstances, when there was no scandal hanging over her head.

She knew good and well what she was thinking— the man had looked amazing standing there in her brother's office. And he'd been polite and almost determined not to intrude in her time with her family, or he simply could have wanted to get away from the odd lady who didn't have the sense to get off the roof and out of the rain.

That could be the case, but still, the anticipation of seeing him again settled over her as she pulled into Shar's driveway and parked. She got out of the Jeep and the cool breeze drifted over her.

She inhaled and looked up at the cotton candy clouds. A seagull flew over as she studied the sky and inhaled the salt air. She enjoyed the California beaches but had been so busy in the heart of LA that she couldn't remember the last time she'd driven down to the water.

Hiding out had its rewards.

Grabbing her purse, she entered the house and kicked her sandals off as she headed for the kitchen and a glass of iced water. She carried it out onto the deck—it was time to enjoy.

There was no one on the beach as she took a drink

of her water. Instead of sitting in the deck chair, she set the water on the table and strode barefoot down the steps and headed down the path to the sand. The water, the surf, and the sudden desire to dip her toes into it drew her. She wore a sundress, so she wasn't concerned with rolling up her pants and immediately she entered the lapping surf. She loved finding seashells and studied the sand for something unique. As she wandered aimlessly down the beach, her thoughts eased and instead of pondering her dilemma, she found herself contemplating BJ.

Shielding her gaze, she studied the homes from the water's edge. They were fairly secluded, sitting slightly off the beach with palms and landscape to protect them from view. That would help if she found a persistent photographer who really wanted to try to invade her privacy. With luck, they would realize she wasn't really news and pull back before something like that happened. However, if not, they would have a bit of a problem figuring out which home she was staying in.

And that was a very good thing.

BJ stared at the phone on the counter beside the pictures he'd been going through. He needed to return the lawyer's calls. He needed to find out more about his past. Needed to start filtering through where he went from here.

But, just like the revelations he'd gotten last week from Gage when he'd learned his mother had hidden his past from him, he knew that the call to the lawyer would reveal and change even more about the life he'd grown comfortable with.

It was inevitable.

But he just couldn't do it. Not yet.

Walking to the large windows overlooking the water, he stared out at the beach. Tugging off his shirt, he left his phone on the counter and headed outside. He was halfway to the water when he saw Olivia.

She sat on a large rock with her chin resting on her knees. Her arms secured her sundress; they were wrapped around her legs while she stared out at the water. The breeze blew strands of her hair about her as she seemed lost in thought. With the sound of the surf, there was no way that she knew he was there.

Not wanting to startle her, he moved closer to the water so that she might see him in her line of vision and then he moved toward her. He'd been hoping to see her again.

He waved. "So we meet again," he called. His adrenaline kicked in when she smiled at him.

"Hi. I wondered if I'd see you again. And just to assure you, I can get off this rock by myself."

Cute. "Glad to hear it. So did you have a good lunch with your family?" His pulse kicked in when she glanced at his bare chest and then yanked her gaze back to the ocean. He reminded himself that she had a man in her life.

"I did. I've missed them." She looked back at him, her gaze locked on his face—much like he'd locked onto her face when she'd been stuck on the roof in those wet pajamas.

He cleared his throat. "So you've been away working?" He was fishing and there was no reason to hide the fact.

"Yes…in LA. I'm in public relations."

"That's a booming business out there, I'd assume anyway."

"If you're good it is."

"I'm sure you are."

Her expression grew troubled. "I thought I was. Now, I'm not so sure. I've gotten myself into a bit of a fix so I'm here sorting it out."

A fix? "So, I don't mean to pry but can't help myself. Are you Brad Pearson's PR person?"

Her eyes narrowed and she grimaced. "You saw the photos?"

"On the way home from town. You looked pretty tight with him. Is it serious?"

"No. It's nonexistent."

"That was nonexistent? Looked like a great kiss." His gaze went to her pretty lips.

"I was blindsided."

"Really? You looked pretty involved."

She scowled. "Like I said, I was startled and that translated to the photo like I was fully engaged in the plan."

Why was he pushing? "Sorry, it's none of my business."

"Believe me, my phone is ringing off the wall. My messages are going crazy and I've been offered large sums of money for a tell-all interview with one of the tabloids, now that they know who I am. It's overwhelming. On the one hand, it's my job to handle things like this but when it's about me, it's a different dynamic. It's overwhelming."

She did look stressed. "Do you want to walk and talk? I've got my own mind-boggling situation going on. The beach is calling to me."

She studied him, and then ran a hand through her hair, trying to calm the flyaways. "I'd love to walk."

He held his hand out to her to help her rise from the rock; when she slipped her hand in his, his pulse skipped and then soared. Much like the excitement he felt when he turned his boat toward open water and headed toward the horizon and the fish he would find.

But Olivia was no fish. No, she was not.

She was as deep and mysterious as the ocean

depths.

He tugged her up from the rock and as she stood up, they were close. As close as they'd been when he'd helped her climb down the ladder.

Once again, the overwhelming desire to wrap his arms around her washed over him. And when she tilted her head to look up at him, he very nearly bent down and kissed her.

He stepped back. His heart thundered as he struggled to focus. *What was wrong with him?* "So, if you two aren't an item, I guess he was taking a shot at winning you over?" *Nothing like being blunt and laying the cards on the table.*

She started to walk and he fell into step with her.

"If that's what that was, it was a really bad move. No, I've been thinking hard about it. He called me and said he needed my help. I only went to the hotel because he'd called about some problem that had happened in the bar the night before. I've been thinking about it and I'm pretty sure I was set up. That the whole thing was a way to get him some attention and I fell right into it."

BJ grinned; he couldn't help it as he realized that Olivia wasn't involved with the actor. That left her wide open on the relationship horizon. And that made him happy. "I'm sorry you were used, but I'm glad you're not his girl."

She halted on the wet sand, her bare feet making footprints before the fingers of surf washed up and over her feet and then receded behind her. BJ had let his gaze drift down her and now looked up and met those alluring eyes again. There were two lines of consternation between her eyebrows.

"I was never his girl. He was my client. And I never envisioned that I'd find myself being the focus of a paparazzi blitz." She looked about. "I'm afraid that today they'll show up and the few hours of relief I've had will go up in smoke. I'm hiding out at Shar's because of the housing situation. Shar doesn't rent this bungalow or own it. She lives here as a housesitter for the absentee owners of the estate. That being the case, I'm a little less traceable here than anywhere else. But Windswept Bay is a small place. I was alerting Levi of the almost inevitable invasion to come since my status as the 'mystery woman' was revealed."

"That's too bad. Why don't you tell them what's going on?"

"I will, but at that moment, it wouldn't have mattered. If I spoke out too soon, they would have just added to the speculation since, as you can guess, they make their money off speculation, lies, and sometimes the truth. Any story about Brad is worth something and it can be twisted and blown up many different ways. Silence from me was my first best defense."

That didn't make sense to him. "But if you'd called him out on it, at least you would have put your story out there."

"It's not that easy. I'm trying to salvage my reputation too, and that's where the majority of my trouble stemmed from. And Brad is calling me. His most recent message was him insisting that he's in love with me. That he has been hiding his feelings."

"Well, at least the guy is showing some smarts on that end."

"Excuse me?"

BJ shrugged. "I've only known you for a short

while but I already know you're a…great person. I can see where he could fall for you."

"Well, thank you."

"Don't look so uncomfortable. I won't start stalking you and the paparazzi won't be coming after you because of me—even if they did snap a photo of me kissing you."

She looked slightly uncomfortable then, hesitation in her eyes, and it only made him want to protect her all the more from the hounds that had her hiding out. And yes, he wanted to kiss her.

She took a deep breath and her gaze shifted to his lips, causing a sharp catch in his chest. *She felt the same pull that he was.* The thought sent his heart thundering against his ribs.

"You have a lot going on in your life too," she said in a sprint and started to walk again. He didn't move at first, letting the attraction bouncing between them settle over him. Yes, he did have a lot going on in his life. And flirting with an attraction between his new brother's sister-in-law might be a little too close to home. But as he took two strides and caught up with

Olivia, he shoved that thought out of the way. He and Olivia were adults and they didn't need anyone's approval but their own where dating came into play.

"I have a few things going on," he said, trying to keep the conversation light. Keeping the darker aspects of his newfound history at bay.

"I'm sure that it was a shock to learn you had a brother. Shar said it was for Gage. But he was and is excited about having someone in his family now. Do you have any other family?"

He had been able to tell in the brief time he'd had around Gage before he and Shar had headed off on their honeymoon that Gage was excited to have him as a brother. BJ was adjusting. "I have to admit that it's a harder acceptance for me. Not that I don't think, at least in the little that I've known Gage, that he's a good man. It's just that, I had a family that I loved. My dad was a great man and suddenly realizing he wasn't my biological dad is unsettling. Learning that my mother kept this from me is even more upsetting. But learning that she took me and ran away and hid me from my biological dad is the most disturbing and unbelievable part. Why? The question won't ease up. Why would she do that?" Feeling bewildered, as he had for days, BJ met Olivia's sympathetic gaze. "It doesn't make sense to me. And yes, I have a sister. Her name is Lilly."

He raked a hand through his hair as all the questions surged forward. *Why was he revealing all of this to Olivia? She had enough on her plate and yes, despite being attracted to her, she was a virtual stranger to him.*

She placed a hand on his arm and stopped him. They were closer to the end of the beach now; there were rocks and the surf was washing up and hitting the rocks. Salty, damp air surrounded them as she smiled gently up at him.

"I suspect all those emotions you're experiencing would be rational and normal right now. I can only speculate how you must feel. I mean, everything you believed about your life has been turned upside down and shaken around like puzzle pieces in a jar."

"That's a perfect metaphor. I haven't even told my sister yet. It's going to be just as surprising to her too."

"Get it straight in your own head and then let her know. I tend to hold things back myself. My family gets frustrated at times but being a triplet—it's always been great, but also a struggle to be my own individual. I hold back bits of myself because of that. But I can tell you I've missed my sisters. My brothers and my parents, too." She didn't blush but she looked shocked. "And here I am telling you this." She groaned softly. "This is so not like me. Please forget everything." She laughed.

"We've both been through a really trying time. Getting you off that roof was a lifelong bonding experience."

A smile burst across her face. "Of course, that explains everything. You saved my life and now you know all my secrets. I'd still be sitting up there if you hadn't shown up because my family had no idea I was here and I didn't have a phone on me."

"That explains it all. And now I know your secrets

and you know mine." As unusual as his life had been since he'd arrived in Windswept Bay, standing here with her felt absolutely right.

"Would you like to go for a boat ride?" he asked, on a whim. He wasn't expecting the look that came over her the moment she heard the question.

CHAPTER FIVE

Olivia was even more startled by his question than she had been by how much about her troubles she'd just revealed to him. But getting on a boat…it had been a long time.

Her stomach dipped at the thought of going out to sea.

"Are you afraid of the water too?" he asked almost immediately and she wondered whether her expression had confused him.

"No, I don't get seasick. I just have a problem with heights. I actually adore the water."

"That's a very good thing. I could sail around the world and be perfectly happy not touching land again, ever."

"Now, I'm not that in love with the water but I used to enjoy going out for a day trip. I was once a decent fisherman."

"A woman after my own heart. This is getting better and better, since I'm a charter boat captain." His lip hitched, enticingly. "Come, take a ride with me. Let your cares go for a little while. I'll take you out early in the morning and bring you back whenever you're ready."

She shouldn't. She needed to hole up and get prepared for when the reporters descended on Windswept Bay...

But then BJ held out his hand. "Come on. Getting out on that perfect blue water will be good for you."

Despite all her reasons for not wanting to go on the water, and there were many, she slipped her hand into his.

Something about BJ magnetized her. Drew her to him, as if drawn by an irresistible force. Her heart beat too rapidly as he smiled at her with excitement shining in his eyes.

She melted instantly as he tugged her gently and they fell into step together, heading back down the beach. He did not let go of her hand and though she knew the right thing was to release his hand, she didn't want to. Everything about BJ told her he was a kind man, a good and honest man. And after dealing with the likes of Brad Pearson, maybe she just needed to wipe that bad memory away by spending time with a man like BJ.

They were several yards down the beach and he released her hand. "I guess I better give your hand back." He grinned and then looked out at the water.

"Thanks."

"I love the water," he said after a few awkward moments in which they walked silently down the beach. "My dad loved the water. He taught me much of what I know and inspired me to carve a career out of what I loved. I've seen much of the world and almost every US port in that boat."

"Really? So you're not ever in one place long?"

"I love to move around. I like not being tied to one place."

"It sounds lonely."

"Not really. I meet people. And I stay along the coast of Florida and the Keys a lot during the year and have made friends everywhere."

"How long do you usually stay in one place?" She wondered how long he'd be in Windswept Bay.

"Not usually more than three to five months at the most. Too much to see and not enough time."

He had a restless or adventurous spirit, she noted. She picked adventurous because nothing about him seemed restless. "I had felt like that once." *A long time ago.*

"Kindred spirits," he commented.

That perfect smile turned sexy enough to turn her knees to mush. Of course, that shirtless chest with his well-toned muscles hadn't helped. She'd been fighting the urge not to stare ever since he'd walked up.

And she was losing the battle.

When they reached the path that led to Shar's bungalow, they stopped. She didn't want the afternoon to end but the idea of spending time on the water with him tomorrow instead of dealing with the tabloids was extremely enticing.

"We can stay out tomorrow as long as you want. I'll pack a lunch and there are facilities in the cabin area."

"I like you more already. I'm not fond of buckets." She chuckled, remembering boat trips as a kid.

A sexy smile slashed across his tanned face. "I'll do whatever it takes to win you over."

"Well, I thank you. I'm sure all clients, especially female fishermen, thank you."

"Right now you're the only one I'm trying to impress."

She laughed. "Well, facilities certainly did the trick."

"Great. Then I'll shoot for the moon. My house has seven bathrooms."

Olivia nearly crumpled over with laughter at the exaggerated look of pride on his face. The man had a great sense of humor. "I am overwhelmed with excitement for you."

"As you should be."

"Sooo," she said, focusing down the beach where the massive, multi-level house stood in the late afternoon sun. It was impossible to make it secluded like the other homes in this section. "Not to change the subject from the fascinating subject that we've been exploring, but I'm curious. The way I understand the situation, Gage came here to get away after his—*your*—father passed away. Only after he was here, he discovered this house had secrets and he found out about you through photos he found inside the house. And then learned at the reading of the will more about you and that you both own the house?"

"*And* share equal ownership of the aforementioned seven bathrooms," BJ added lightly. "Yes, confusing as heck but that about sums it up. Or at least that's my understanding of the situation. I'm supposed to fly out to New York and meet the lawyer and hear the details. Problem is, I have not one bit of interest in flying into that overpopulated city and being hemmed in by all those skyscrapers. Not when my life is on open water."

Olivia had an *ah-ha* moment. "You are afraid of congested cities."

"You are not the only one with hang-ups." He grinned delightfully.

Olivia's own smile began to widen automatically. "Wow, and you even admitted it. I like that. No macho man denial."

He hitched a shoulder. "No—with me, you get what you see. I'm comfortable in my own skin and I don't like cities. At least not the heart of cities. At least not those with buildings so tall and tightly located that the only way to see the sky is by riding an elevator to the top or being satisfied with a strip of sky the width of the street. Me not being there just leaves more room for the people who love them. I'm just not going there."

"I completely see the logic in your thinking. I feel the same way about rooftops. From here on out, I will not under any circumstances climb up there."

"See, we understand each other. I better go. I'll meet you at the dock at six. Is that too early? The water's great at that time."

"I'll be ready." She watched him walk away while butterflies played in her chest. Earlier, she'd been dreading tomorrow and what it held for her but now, she couldn't wait for the sun to come up.

BJ liked her and found himself whistling as he strode down the sand toward the monstrosity of a house at the curve of the beach. He liked the way Olivia thought, the way she teased, the way she looked with her blonde hair and alert green eyes, and her totally unassuming air. Olivia was a woman who knew herself and was comfortable in her skin. At least for the most part.

He could tell from the little she'd talked about it that this deal with the paparazzi coming after her, instead of after her clientele, had shaken her up. But she was getting her feet back under her and maybe a day on the water would be just the boost she needed. At least it would relax her; he'd make sure of that.

Time on the water could help a lot of things. It was the place where he thought the best. It was the place that he loved and he was excited to share it with

Olivia. Tomorrow would be a good day.

No, tomorrow would be a *great* day.

"I've missed this," Olivia called over the rushing wind, the next morning as they cut through the water at a fast, but safe speed. They were cruising across the blue water toward several small islands and the sun was still soft and new on the early morning horizon.

The boat was large enough that the spray from the water didn't splatter over them but Olivia wouldn't have minded if it had. She loved it.

"I'm glad you're enjoying it," BJ called from the captain's chair next to her, his words buffeted by the wind.

The wind whipped his curls across his forehead, giving him a happy, youthful look. It made her realize as she smiled at him that he carried a more serious attitude in his expression when on land. It was obvious the ocean was where his heart was. Right now, with the wind in his face, he looked exuberant.

"Oh." She stared across the bay toward the

71

mangroves that grew off the coast like barrier shrubs. "Head that way and I may be able to share something really cool with you. If it is still there after all these years."

"Sure thing." He immediately turned the boat toward the mangroves. As they approached, the water grew more shallow and she knew he wouldn't be able to get as close to them as smaller boats but still, he'd be able to see her surprise.

Here in the shallows, the water was very calm and completely clear. The rock and sand at the bottom could be seen and there wasn't a fish in sight for the most part. They were hiding in the mangrove roots that were a tangled mass above and beneath the water's surface. Then the nurse sharks appeared. Small ones, flat and nearly white in the water as they darted out from the extensive root system. "I always think mangroves are pretty creepy." She laughed. "I mean, they grow out here in the shallows with all their roots and you have no idea what is living in there among them. Like these sharks. The first time I saw these when I was young, it really shocked me. Because I thought it looked like you could jump into the water and swim, and many people do, but this girl doesn't. Have I mentioned that I am not a fan of sharks? Even baby nurse sharks. You never see the moms but I can't help thinking that they are near."

"I hear you. It's not nurse sharks that keep me in the boat."

"Me either. There." She spied the opening in the mangroves that she thought was right. It had been years, but she'd come here often back then. "Can you get through that channel? I believe if you stay in the middle, it's deep enough for this boat and you'll get through to the far side."

"Can do. And if not, I don't mind being stuck here with you," he teased.

"I believe you're a flirt," she shot back as he maneuvered through the rows of green bushes until the channel opened up and they were on the other side of the maze of mangroves.

"I have my moments," he agreed.

She sat up as she spotted it. "There." She pointed across the expanse. "Do you see it?"

"Hey, it's an eagle's nest." Excitement vibrated in his words.

She smiled and felt the excitement fill her too. "I first discovered it when I was in high school. Isn't it cool? The eagle comes back here every year to have her babies. I'm sure because of storms she's had to rebuild a few times. But the mangroves protect it."

Because the gnarly trees were short and squat, the nest was only about six feet above the water. It sat among the limbs like a cone.

"The mangroves help the ecosystem and are essential to the environment. This is just another example of their value."

"You sure know a lot about the environment."

"I used to research them," she admitted. "Back when I thought I would go into some type of career that would have to do with the ecosystem."

He stared at her. "So, you are an enigma, Miss Sinclair. You thought you might go into a career involving the ecological system but instead you ended up in Hollywood protecting the rights of movie stars. Why do the two choices not jive at all?"

She looked down and then away, avoiding his gaze. She hadn't spoken of her career choice in a very long time. "I just decided along the way that I was better suited to deal with Hollywood."

Tilting his head, he studied her, as if seeing all her secrets. She fought hard not to convey any emotion.

"Why can't I believe it's that simple?" he mused, after a moment.

They had known each other a short time and yet he was reading her like a biography. She shot him an irritated look. "You don't have to believe it."

He looked mildly abashed. "Okay, so you're saying back off. That'll really make me believe you're not hiding something."

The man was irritating. "Look, I just don't want to talk about it."

"Why?"

"Are you always this obnoxious and nosey?"

"Not really." He gave a small, dismissive laugh. "But you obviously love the water, love the small details that make the environment work, and yet you chose to go be a publicist in Hollywood and deal with jerks who can't take care of their own dirty laundry. I'm baffled. But interested. Very interested. As in you interest me. If I haven't made that clear." He smiled and her bad mood softened.

He really was interested, she realized. Her family had once pressed her to find out why she'd made the choices she'd made and they'd stopped after she'd pushed back. He hadn't pushed back. They'd understood that once she made her mind up there was no changing it. BJ hadn't known her long enough to know that about her. *You interest me.* His words echoed through her.

He had slowed the boat and was steering it clear of the shallows, but now he angled the boat toward the open water just past the mangroves.

She sat down for the ride toward open water.

He smiled over at her. "Don't be mad at me."

She laughed because she couldn't help it. "Okay, I'm not mad. But you see too much. Push too hard and are nosey as all get-out. If I don't want to talk about something, then I don't want to talk about it."

"Fine. Be that way." He laughed and pulled back

on the throttle. Instantly the boat responded with a powerful growl as the engines kicked in with speed.

"What about you?" she pressed, feeling it was her turn to be nosey. *Fair was fair.* "Are you any closer to knowing why your mother ran away with you?"

"Any closer than I was yesterday? Nope. Not a bit."

"I find that very baffling."

"Tell me about it."

She smiled at him, despite still being mildly irritated at his prying. "So, did you think about your situation anymore last night? Are you going to fly to New York and see the lawyer?"

"Nope. I called him this morning and told him to pack his bags and catch a plane down here and share the details with me."

"And he said okay, just like that?"

"I persuaded him when I told him I'd take him out on the boat. Can you believe that New York lawyer has never taken a fishing vacation? I told him he did not know what he was missing and that I could assure him that he would catch a whole host of deep sea fish if he came out. Tuna, mahi, and if he got here by next week, we'd get him a marlin and possibly a wahoo."

She was stunned. "And he took the bait?"

BJ grinned. "Like a big daddy Goliath grouper."

She laughed, hard. "You are a genius."

"Nope. I just know how to fish." There was only about twelve inches separating them as BJ smiled at her with twinkling eyes. His blue eyes were expressive, very pressing and probing at one moment—piercing, icy-blue. But now they shifted to softer blue that twinkled as he grinned that sexy, totally engaging smile at her.

And she wondered suddenly whether he were fishing right now. *For her.*

The idea stole her breath.

And then he let off the throttle. The boat instantly coasted as he turned and cupped her jaw. The boat rocked as he very gently brushed his thumb across her cheek.

And she was caught—hook, line, and sinker.

CHAPTER SIX

BJ couldn't help himself as he touched Olivia's soft cheek. This had been what he'd thought would be a relaxing day. Instead, it had turned unexpectedly to their problems. But it was okay because Olivia had things on her mind that she needed to get off. And he was very curious about what he had learned about her.

The expression on her face when she talked about the mangroves and about the sharks and about the ocean had been unlike anything prior to that. She'd lit up in a beautiful way.

Not that she wasn't already beautiful. No doubt about it—he could look at her all day. Who was he kidding? He could look at her for the rest of his life. It was true. But when she'd started talking about the beauty around them, something in her had engaged him on a deeper level.

He'd been around a lot of women in his lifetime but none of them moved him like Olivia.

Everything about her pulled him in and it was as if he could sense and feel what she was thinking. Feeling.

As if they were connected.

Likewise, she could almost read him like a book. It was an unnerving feeling. She was probably trying to get back at him because he was prying into her life.

But right now he wanted to kiss her.

She didn't move as he looked down at her lips and then gently he slipped his hand to the back of her neck and tugged her toward him. His heart thundered in his chest and he could see in her eyes that she felt it too. At least he thought—hoped—the feeling was mutual.

"You are mesmerizing," he said softly and then he lowered his lips to hers.

As his lips melted to Olivia's, emotions and feelings drove through him. When she returned the kiss, his chest tightened, his heart thundered harder, and the sweet sensation of perfection wrapped them in a sweet cocoon, as if only the two of them existed in the world.

He pulled back. Stunned, he breathed hard. She looked just as dazed as he felt. They stared at each other. He had absolutely no idea what to say. He had never had or felt that connection before. He'd never wanted that connection before…the kind that tied him to one place. Docked him indefinitely.

Olivia was special and there was nothing about meeting her that was ordinary. Something about being with her made him feel as though his life would never be the same.

"I am not sure that was a good idea," he managed to say at last, glad he sounded somewhat coherent. He needed to take this slow and figure out where it was going. He couldn't bear it if he hurt her.

She blinked at him. Her brows knit together. "You might be right," she said. "Although, at least there are no paparazzi around."

He laughed, easing the tension. "At least we hope not."

A heartbeat of silence stretched between them before he nodded toward her chair. "Have a seat and hang on. We're going to deep water."

In more ways than one, he thought, as he pushed the throttle forward and sent the boat flying across the waves.

Off the Florida coast, the tropical tones of teal and sea foam cascaded together like puzzle pieces as the shallow water slowly faded into the deeper jewel tones of jade and sapphire. It was a beauty Olivia loved. And had missed.

The open water and the warm, salty breeze called to Olivia. The scents of seaweed and fresh air filled her lungs, making it a perfect moment. But even that did not rank with the amazing sensation of BJ's lips on hers. The kiss had launched the beauty and wonder of this day into the stratosphere.

Her heart hammered erratically as they crossed the water. "It has been so long since I've been out on the water," she called over the rushing air. Once she loved open water and she'd loved deep sea fishing. She'd eaten it up, loved everything about the life: snorkeling, fishing, wave runners, windsurfing…and she'd also loved Adam Davies.

She hadn't thought of Adam in a long time. She hadn't wanted to.

Adam had been everything to her all through high school and when they'd gone off to college with plans to spend their lives together, life was perfect. Or so she believed.

"Why not?" BJ asked. "If you love it, why have you stayed away from it? Seriously." His hair whipped across his forehead as their eyes met.

"A lot of reasons," she hedged, finding it unnerving looking at him and realizing she wanted to kiss him again. "Nothing I really want to talk about." *They'd just gone over this and already he was prying again.*

She studied the water, hoping to see dolphins

running along with them that might change the subject for her.

She hoped he'd let the topic go because he'd awakened something inside her that she hadn't felt in a long time. Not since Adam, and he was the last person she wanted to think about right now…but she did.

Adam had planned to become a marine biologist and she had planned on being an ecologist. They'd dreamed of traveling the world together. And then their senior year in college, out of nowhere, Adam had revealed that there was someone else in his life. And in one fell swoop, he had moved on.

He'd taken their dreams with him and shared their life with his new love.

She'd learned that he had been seeing his new love for a year and Olivia had been clueless. *Clueless.* It was humiliating on so many levels.

Devastated, furious, and embarrassed, Olivia had told no one.

She couldn't pursue the life that she'd planned after that. Her heart hadn't been in it.

She had applied every credit that she could toward

her new degree in public relations. She was good with words and with people, so she thought it was a good fit.

"Why did you go into PR work?"

She could answer that. "Having been raised in a large family, I learned to be diplomatic and a problem solver. I thought it was a good fit." She repeated some of what she'd been thinking, just not all of it. "One did not have five brothers and three sisters and not know how to talk. Or be diplomatic at times." Olivia smiled. It was also an easy way out of college without telling her parents how devastated she'd been over Adam. Instead, she just told them that they had grown apart as her life headed in a new direction. She suspected that they knew more—she was positive that her sisters knew something had happened—but she was adamant that she was pursuing a career that she loved.

"Do you love it?" He sounded skeptical, considering he'd made his views on her clientele known earlier.

"It excited me, at least in the beginning." And it actually had. "Now it's becoming tiresome," she said, truthfully. "And this problem with Brad hasn't helped the situation." *It might have even given her the excuse to leave Hollywood and come home for a little while.* The thought struck her out of nowhere.

The revelation was startling.

"Time to fish," BJ called when he saw a gathering of seagulls ahead of them. Birds hovering over the water meant fish, lots of fish, and he could see that Olivia was not happy about whatever she was thinking about. Dropping the anchor, he headed to the rods. He wanted to ease her mind and give her a carefree day. Not stress her out more. He smiled and waggled the rod at her. "Are you ready to dip a hook in the water?"

"I am. As a boat captain, I wondered if it sometimes grew old to you. But you look like a kid in a candy store right now."

He shot her a big, wide grin. "I chose this business because I love it. It never grows old. I can fish all day, every day, for the rest of my life. Don't get me wrong: I do enjoy other things, but this is my dream job. My dream life."

It was all true.

"That's wonderful. Not many people can say that."

"Yeah, I know. I don't take it for granted." He motioned for her to come get the rod. "It's ready. Let's bring 'em in."

He was excited to see the excitement in her expression as she moved to take the rod. Their hands touched and the spark of what he'd come to know was their chemistry fired through him. She swallowed hard as her fingers wrapped around the handle and he let go. *This was about fishing, not kissing. Or the want to kiss her.*

He watched her expertly handle the rod and he was impressed that she knew what she was doing. "I can tell this isn't your first rodeo."

She laughed. "Fishing I know. Rodeos are another story."

He chuckled and loved her laughter. "No cowgirl or rodeo lover hidden in there like your brother Cam?"

"No. Cam just always knew from early on that he

wanted to be a cowboy. It was the weirdest thing for him to live on the coast and always know he'd be on a horse when he grew up. My parents made sure we all had riding lessons at the small stables just down the road from the resort. But like rooftops, I didn't take to riding so well. Fishing I loved from the start."

Then why, he wondered again, *had she stopped?* It was baffling but something in her expression earlier had told him she had memories she wasn't talking about.

"Don't get me wrong." He picked up his own fishing rod. "I enjoy spending time with a beautiful woman too. That's why today is perfect. I've got fishing and a beautiful woman all in the same moment."

"You're a charmer," she said, giving a cute snort that made him laugh. "So how did you get into this career?"

"My dad loved it. He was a big fisherman. I can still remember the trips we took when I was a child. He loved it. But we only did it a few times in my lifetime. One day while we were on the water, I can remember him telling me that if there was any career that he could have chosen, it would have been a sea captain. He'd not been raised around water and had come to love it later in life. Long after he'd become an accountant."

"I was going to ask what his profession was."

"Accountant extraordinaire. He was very good at what he did. He liked it okay, but it wasn't fishing. When he was on the water, it was like you were earlier—alive, excited. When you started talking about it and when we got the water beneath us, you sparkled, Olivia. He did the same thing. When he and my mom died, those memories of him knowing what made him happy put me on the path to the life I have today. I chose this life because of him. And it's brought me a lot of happiness."

And it had brought him in to Windswept Bay and to Olivia.

Like the warmth of sunshine on a spring day, the knowledge settled over him. It was true.

But would it hold him? Could staying in one spot fulfill him?

CHAPTER SEVEN

Olivia tilted her head and watched him. "Contentment," she said. He was the most content man she'd ever met and that was something that drew her to him. "I've sensed that in you from the first moment I met you."

Her stomach trembled as his gaze lingered on her face.

"So that's my question to you," he said. "Why you loved something so much and yet you walked away from it?"

"You are persistent." It was irritating but also nice

that he seemed so interested in her. Really interested that he kept fishing over and over again for her to open up to him.

"I am when it comes to something I care about and, Olivia, I've already told you I care about you."

They stared at each other as the boat bobbed in the water. He glanced away to scan where they were fishing, and then he put his gaze back on her and she was riveted to him.

She wasn't ready to open up and yet she was drawn to him. "You never finished telling me how you became a boat captain."

She wanted to take the conversation away from her but she really wanted to know everything about him.

"When my dad and my mom passed away, I remembered what my dad had said and I chose to do what I longed to do. When I was able to, I took the money I inherited and I bought my boat. Then I headed this way. I actually spent a lot of time down in the Keys in Marathon and across the Seven Mile Bridge in the waters around Bahia Hondo National Park, taking people tarpon fishing. People will pay to learn to catch a tarpon and other fighting fish in the waters around there. Good memories gave me a good place to begin my business. Lilly went with me and volunteered at the park for a while before heading off to follow her own path. We both needed time there, though. She still goes down periodically and volunteers at the park."

"It sounds like it's a very important place to you both. I love that area too," Olivia agreed. "Once, my dad took all of us down there and we stayed in one of the little cabins in the park for two weeks. It was an amazing, busy place but we were able to run around the area and ride our bikes around the island, swim and fish all we wanted to."

"Your memories of it sound like mine."

"Weird, isn't it? So where is your sister now?"

"She went into the field that she adored too, living a nomad's life—going from one wildlife park to another, working and seeing the country. She's in Yellowstone right now, I think. I can't keep up with her. It's time for me to call her and check in. We both have what I call restless spirits."

And she'd marked that off earlier. *He was restless.* Suddenly, her line started to spin out of control. "I've got something!"

"Oh yeah, here we go," he called, and moved beside her.

Olivia was smiling as she looked up at him, excitement and adrenaline racing inside her as if she'd just been caught in an electrical storm. "Now, this is fun."

"A woman after my own heart," he said, his eyes bright with excitement.

Olivia's knees weakened and she almost forgot about the fish on the end of her line. This trip home had taken an unexpected turn and Olivia suddenly didn't care whether this day ever ended.

Everything about it was perfect.

And then her phone rang.

The sound startled Olivia and she jerked her line. Instantly it snapped and the large fish on the other end was gone. She'd never even glimpsed what it was.

"No way," Olivia yelped in dismay. "I've been too many places on the mainland where there was no phone service or terrible phone service but here, fifteen miles offshore, I can receive calls."

"I should have gotten us a little farther offshore." BJ gave an apologetic grimace that made her smile as she pulled the phone from her pocket.

"Maybe so but this is Levi and if he couldn't reach me, he might have thought something was wrong so it's for the best." She hit Accept and put the phone to her ear. "Hello—"

"Where are you?" Levi barked, without any kind of hello.

No question about it, he was irritated. "I'm actually fishing. I'm out on the boat with BJ."

"Fishing," he growled. "Well, I hate to interrupt your day but your entourage has arrived."

"My entourage." She almost laughed—which would have been an obvious mistake given the seriousness of her brother's voice. He was absolutely in no mood for humor. "Where did you learn that word?" she asked, keeping the laughter out of her voice.

"Hey, I'm not in the mood. These people are ridiculous. You need to get back here. They are pretty much everywhere, asking questions and trying to figure out where you are."

An hour ago, the news would have upset her. Now, she looked over at BJ and at the moment, it didn't seem as big a deal any longer.

"Olivia, are you still there?"

"Yes, sorry, Levi. What were you saying?"

"That these people piling up like flies outside the resort are causing all kinds of uproar. I do not get it."

Olivia chuckled. "Levi, a photo is worth a lot of money to them. It's their job. Brad is hot news right now with his new movie being the top release. A photo could mean five figures or higher to them."

"You're telling me that somebody would pay ten thousand or so for photos of you?"

"Well, wow, Levi. You don't think a picture of me is worth that much?" She couldn't help teasing him.

"I don't think anybody's photo is worth ten thousand. But I think you're worth more than money could buy."

"Good answer," she said, touched.

"The only answer as far as I'm concerned, sis. Now could you get back here so we can figure out what our next move is going to be? I want to make sure you're safe from these jerks. Cali said some of them are being really rude and obnoxious and they're tromping through Jillian's flowers like they're weeds. I don't trust them. Me, Jake, and Trent are waiting at Shar's place for you. Max would be here but he got called away on a mission last night."

She cringed. Max loved his special ops career in the military but it always worried her.

"You're at Shar's?" she asked, pushing worry for Max to the prayer room of her heart.

"Yes. Is that a problem? So you're with BJ?"

She hated that she'd just added this big mess to his already tough job as police chief.

"Yes, I'm with BJ. I'll have him bring me back."

"Why am I not surprised you're with him?"

"Um, I'm not sure, but is that a problem?" she asked, copying his words from moments before.

"No, not at all."

"Good. We'll be there shortly." She hung up.

BJ had already reeled in the lines and stored the poles while Olivia was talking. Now he moved to the steering wheel and waited for her to take her seat.

"I guess you figured out that I've been summoned back ashore."

"I kind of got that one figured out. Hang on and fill me in on the rest as we roll."

"Sure. The reporters are there," she added.

"And Levi's worried about you."

It wasn't a question, she realized. He was stating a fact, as if he understood.

"Yes. He wants to get us to get our plan of action figured out."

"Good. Whatever it takes to keep you safe."

"They're just reporters. I've never been afraid of them, just didn't want to answer questions."

"And they've come a long way for a story, which tells me, and probably Levi, that they want a story pretty badly. It doesn't hurt to be cautious and prepared."

"Then it's time to head back." She sank back in the seat, realizing she was more upset that her day with BJ was ending than she was about the fiasco that was brewing back on shore.

The dock was loaded down with Sinclair men when BJ pulled up to it.

Olivia's dad Sam was there, along with Levi, Jake, and Trent. He wasn't sure where Max was but BJ knew Cam had headed back to Texas after Gage and Shar's wedding. He'd only spent a little time with Olivia's family but it looked as though the family was ready to take on the world for her. BJ liked that and would be joining them. No one was going to hurt or insult Olivia while he was around.

These so-called journalists better tread carefully because they hadn't done themselves any favors by splashing her name and her good reputation across the front of their trash magazines and then following her across the country to her home turf.

"They don't look happy," he said.

Olivia groaned and rubbed her forehead. "No. They look ready to fight. What have I gotten my family into?"

He shot her a frown. "Nothing. It's not your fault. You didn't ask Brad to grab you on the street and kiss you for the cameras." He slowly pulled the boat close to the dock and then went to toss Jake a line. "Thanks, man," he called.

"Anytime." Jake caught the line and bent to one knee to tie the boat to the dock. "I'm just glad to know Olivia was with you."

"Yeah," Trent called, snagging the back of the boat and taking the rope BJ handed him. "With all the jerks roaming around looking for her, it's good to know she was with you."

BJ started to say he was too but Olivia spoke first.

"He took me fishing. I didn't need to be looked out for."

"Says you," Jake shot back.

"We see it different," Trent added, tersely.

Exasperation lit Olivia's expression but instead of saying more to her obviously determined brothers, she turned her attention to her dad, who held out his hand to her.

"Dad, you haven't been worried, have you?" Olivia looked up at her dad and accepted his help from the boat.

"Yes, I have. There are a dozen or more men staked outside the resort looking for you and I don't know how many more are roaming around in the bushes waiting to jump out and harass you. Not to mention the ones staked out across the road from our house." He pulled her into his arms. "It's good to have you home. Even if the circumstances are not to my liking, I'm glad you came home to us."

She wrapped her arms around his waist and BJ saw the love on her face as she hugged her dad. "I'm sorry to make you worry."

"Not your fault," he said—exactly what BJ had told her. "Now let's see what we can do to fix all this ridiculousness." His serious gaze met BJ's over her head. "They don't know she's here at Shar's yet. But I'm glad you were around today in case one of them had shown up."

"I'm glad I'm around too."

Olivia turned to her brothers. "Sorry, guys. Thanks to all of you for coming."

Levi nodded and finally spoke. "You did a good thing choosing to come to Shar's place because it's harder to get her address since she's just housesitting here."

"It's a good thing too," Jake agreed. "They've been snooping around my dive shop and Trent's seen them too."

"One trailed me when I was heading out of the construction site to check in with my guys this morning," Trent said. "He didn't like it when I told him he was trespassing and showed him the exit." He grinned cockily and BJ had a feeling the photographer didn't hang around long.

Trent chuckled. "Then another one followed me to the trails and tried to follow me." He grinned. "I took them on a nice long goose chase."

Olivia laughed and smiled at BJ. "He's an ex-Navy SEAL. He can run for days, I think."

BJ laughed. "Well played, man."

Trent shrugged. "It was fun anyway."

The sound of a helicopter had them all turning to stare down the beach.

BJ saw it in the distance flying low along the coastline. "I hope that's just the Coast Guard doing their job making their daily trips up and down the coast. But just in case, maybe we better get Olivia into the house."

"He's right," Levi agreed. "Everyone start moving just in case that bird isn't a friend."

Sam and BJ flanked Olivia as they headed off the dock and across the sand.

"All of you go ahead." Jake jogged past them and plopped into a beach chair. "I'll wait on it." He tugged off his dark-blue tropical shirt, exposing some serious washboard abs to go along with his swim trunks. "I want to see if it's one of my Coast Guard buddies or one of Olivia's hounds."

"When you find out, come up to the house," Levi demanded. "And behave."

"Hey, I'm just a guy getting a tan. And for my own personal reasons, I'm hoping it's that new female recruit who got to town last week. Then again, when she gets a load of these abs, she might ditch the chopper in the ocean accidently."

"I said behave," Levi growled over his shoulder and Jake just laughed.

"Okay, okay." Jake chuckled.

Olivia looked at BJ and just shook her head.

"Brothers," was all she said but her lip twitched upward.

They made it to the bungalow. She stalked up the steps like a woman on a mission and he wondered what was going through her mind.

CHAPTER EIGHT

Olivia turned to the men she loved, and BJ, the man she'd begun to care for in the short time they'd known each other.

"Okay, guys," she said, firmly. "You all have me afraid you're ready to wage war on the photographers. I'll handle this. It's what I do in my day job."

"Not anymore." Levi pointed to the kitchen counter, where there was a stack of tabloids spread across the countertop.

Olivia's heart sank when she caught one of the banners that read "Behind the Scenes of Brad Pearson and Olivia Sinclair's Love Affair." Her mouth fell open in dismay at photos of Brad and a woman entering a hotel. The woman's face couldn't be seen but she had a similar build to Olivia. "That's not even me," she muttered and then snatched up another tabloid with the headline, "Olivia Sinclair Dumped by PR Firm over Affair with Brad Pearson."

"I don't know how it's done in Hollywood but here we take care of our own and we aren't letting you face that alone."

"Levi, I get it. I need to make a phone call before you start locking up everyone who carries a camera."

BJ leaned against the kitchen counter and hadn't said anything. As she pulled her phone from her pocket and walked past him toward her bedroom, he put a hand on her arm.

"Are you okay?" he asked gently.

She nodded, all too aware of the way his touch made her want to suddenly throw herself into his arms. "I'm fine." She moved past him and headed toward her room.

"We are just trying to protect you," Levi called,

clearly frustrated.

"I can protect myself," she snapped, losing patience. She shut her bedroom door and locked it.

Immediately, she dialed her boss, Kate. She should have done it right after the scandal begun. There was a clear-cut policy that getting mixed up with a client was not allowed but Kate knew Olivia wouldn't step over that line. She knew the accusations were false.

Kate answered after the second ring.

"Kate, have you seen the tabloids?"

"Yes, and unfortunately it's true. He's our biggest client and as much as I like you, Olivia, our firm represents him. I can't lose his account."

Olivia's heart sank. She knew what Kate was saying was true and suddenly she didn't even care. "Right. Of course you can't."

"It's just business, Olivia."

The urge to say something that she knew she would regret was strong, so she bit her tongue and held back bitter words and simply said, "They're all lies and you know it."

Olivia felt the sting of tears but dashed them away with the back of her hand. She understood Kate really had no other choice but it still hurt. She'd done her job well and to have it taken away for something completely out of her control and false did not sit well.

"We both know people, especially celebrities, will sometimes do odd things to get attention."

"True. Even so, this seems really out of the ballpark for Brad." She also knew that without him around, she wasn't much of a news story. "This will go away. I'm too far from Hollywood at the moment and the longer these guys camp out in Windswept Bay, the lower their income gets. They won't stay long."

"That's true. Is that why you went so far away?"

Olivia thought about that for a second. "Part of the reason. But I honestly didn't think about that until today. Subconsciously I knew being away from the noise would help me. At least that's what I'm hoping. But part of me was ready to come home. It's time for me to rethink where my life is going and what I want out of it. So it's okay, Kate." She realized suddenly that it was.

"It's still not making me happy."

Kate was a shrewd businesswoman and in the end, it came down to the fact that her business was tied to how she and the company performed for their clients. It was a sad truth. If she chose to support Olivia, she would lose the trust of her client roster and her business would go down the tubes like Olivia's career just had.

"Good luck," was all Olivia said and ended the call. She stared out the window and saw Jake making his way toward the house.

A knock sounded on her bedroom door. "Olivia," Levi said. "We really need to talk about this."

With a sigh, she went to open the door. "Fine. Let's talk it through." She walked past him, back into the kitchen and on into the living room.

Jake came in. "It was the Coast Guard. So your secret is still safe. I, on the other hand, just might have a date tonight."

"You wish," Trent muttered.

"Cut it out, you two," Levi snapped. "What's on your mind, Olivia?"

She scanned the group. "Here it is, guys. I am not much of a story alone. Without Brad beside me, the paparazzi won't stay here long. They need photos they can sell to get their paychecks. Following around Hollywood celebrities pays better than following around boring real people. So dollars will be the deciding factor here. Therefore, I've decided that I will be myself. I'll be visible by going about my daily routine. They'll soon get bored and hungry and head back where the money is."

BJ looked as if he were ready to eat nails. "What if they get rough? You know that's possible. They might push you or corner you. Or try to provoke you to anger," he continued. "You're not going around alone and that's final."

BJ's emphatic, protective statement did not go unnoticed by Olivia—and she was certain all of her brothers or her dad either.

All eyes turned to BJ. His gaze was unwavering as he watched her. The statement had sent a thrill racing through her.

"I refuse to be scared of the paparazzi." She clung

to her independence despite enjoying the knowledge that he wanted to protect her. "I've made statements on behalf of clients many times. I've used them before when I needed tidbits of information leaked out. They just sometimes tend to get overzealous and it isn't a good situation. That has not happened with me."

Every one of the men in her family balked at her statement.

"Not happening," Levi grunted.

Her dad did not look happy. "There are enough of us that you shouldn't need to go out alone."

"But—"

"What if I take you out to dinner?" BJ said. "We'll let the paparazzi see you and take a few photos of me escorting you around. Might even give them a new story for ole sad Brad."

Levi slapped him on the shoulder. "Best idea I've heard today."

And so, just like that, it was settled.

BJ picked her up for dinner and they headed toward

town. She'd wanted to be mad that she'd been railroaded into this date but she wasn't. She was looking forward to spending time with BJ and despite the fact that she loved her family, being with BJ, in this situation, had given her a way to keep some control over it. The fact that she wanted to be near him and spend the evening with him was a plus. And the fact that he wanted to be near her set a warm glow inside her.

The first thing she saw as they neared the resort was the cluster of paparazzi on the corner, with their cameras waiting. Her stomach knotted upon seeing them. *Why was that?* They'd never made her nervous before, but then, the story hadn't involved her then. Her name had never been the one splashed across the headlines. Her privacy had never been encroached upon before and it gave her a new perspective into what her clients had experienced. It was disconcerting and that was undeniable.

"Where would you like to go for dinner?" BJ asked, as if this was a normal evening out.

She laughed at his casual inquiry and it eased

111

some of the tension she was experiencing. "Great question." He'd stopped at the red light within view of the resort. "We could go to the resort or we could go down the street to Casablanca."

"But they are waiting for you at the resort and this is about getting you seen, isn't it?"

Disappointment waved over her at his words. "Yes, you're right. The resort it is. My sisters will get some publicity out of this at least."

"I hear there's some really good restaurants there."

"Yes, Mom and Dad always made certain the food was excellent and my sisters have continued that practice. Windswept Bay Resort is a destination resort not only for its hospitality but for its cuisine." It was true. "Maybe the one overlooking the beach would be a good one for us. It's casual but has great atmosphere and we'd be visible from the beach to our onlookers."

He smiled. "It sounds perfect. Let's do this and really give them something to talk about."

She was startled by his statement. "Okay," she said, not exactly certain what he had on his mind. The twinkle in his eye as he drove forward when the light turned green made her a bit nervous. "I hope you know they don't need *too* much extra to talk about."

He laughed and turned in to the resort drive. "Are you chickening out?"

"No. I'm just not sure what you're thinking."

"That I'm about to take a beautiful woman to dinner on a romantic moonlit evening under the stars."

"Oh." His words sent excitement skipping through her.

"And I'll be cautious, I promise. We will play this by ear."

He pulled beneath the portico and immediately the Windswept Bay doormen opened their doors and welcomed them to the resort. Before anything else could be said, someone shouted her name and the stampede started as all the cameramen charged through the bushes and flower beds. One even jumped a stack of suitcases, trying to be first to reach her. Immediately, he jammed his camera in her face and started flashing as he shouted questions at her.

The doorman got shoved out of the way by another man and his camera. Within seconds, Olivia was backed up against the open door with no way out of the crowd.

"How does it feel to have the whole country focused on you as Brad Pearson's woman?"

"Is it true you're carrying his baby?"

"What?" she snapped, trying to focus on the person who'd asked the ridiculous question.

"How long has the affair been going on?" someone else shouted.

She knew the business, knew how they acted, but this was the first time that they were focused on her. It was overwhelming.

BJ had rushed around the car and now forced himself through the crowd. "Get back," he growled, elbowing them roughly to the side as he reached her and blocked her from their reach. "Back it up right now or someone's about to get tossed across this car."

"Who are you?"

"That's a threat."

"You're right, it is. And not an empty one. Now move back."

Emotion welled inside her at his defense of her.

She couldn't find any words as he settled beside her when they'd been granted the space he'd demanded. She looked up at him; his expression was fierce as he draped a muscled arm over her shoulders.

"Are you okay?" he asked gently and she nodded, wanting only one thing in that moment and that was to kiss him. "Good. Sorry—they threw me off guard with their stampede."

"It's okay," she finally managed. "You got here and I'm glad you're with me."

"I wouldn't have it any other way." He leaned down to whisper in her ear. "You can do this. I'm just your support."

She smiled and loved the way his warm breath feathered over her skin. She looked into his eyes as he pulled back and smiled. She could hear the cameras clicking away but she did not care.

"Hey, who are you?" a man asked, taking a step forward and snapping a close-up.

"I'm the guy who doesn't enjoy having your camera stuffed up my nostrils. Now step back," BJ snapped.

"Hey man, don't get ugly—"

"We'll keep this civil if you keep your distance. I have no problem taking your cameras. Miss Sinclair will answer questions if she feels like it. If she doesn't, we'll get on with our dinner date. Now give the lady some room."

"Hey, we have a job to do."

"And did I say I cared about your job?" BJ countered. "I only care about Olivia."

Olivia's heart raced at his words and though she didn't look up at him, she could visualize the icy warning in his eyes as the cameramen all kept their distance. *This was intense.*

She held up her hand. "Okay, everyone calm down. I'll speak to you. I'll answer one question at a time, if I can. But I will tell you that there is nothing between me and Brad Pearson. I'm not exactly sure why Brad chose to kiss me that day or why he's continued to say things that are clearly only figments of his own creative mind. He has his reasons, of which I am not privy to. For those answers, you'll have to ask him. And he is not here."

"Why were you with him at that hotel?"

"Many of you know I was simply his media rep, his media liaison. We were consulting over the state of his excessive party experience of the night before. That was it. As much as all of you were startled by that kiss that day, I was too. As I've told my family and friends, that kiss blindsided me and meant absolutely nothing to me. Or to him. Contrary to what he'd like you to believe."

"What do you mean, blindsided you?"

"Exactly that. It came out of nowhere. There is nothing romantic between us."

She almost laughed at the disbelieving looks on the reporters' faces.

"We're supposed to believe you were in that hotel room with him and *nothing* was going on. Yeah, right."

Instantly, BJ pulled her snugly against him. "I don't like your attitude," he challenged the speaker.

Olivia rested her hand on his chest and patted him. She looked up at him and smiled, hoping to calm him down and stop drawing so much attention. She didn't need a fistfight on the front pages of the tabloids.

Flashbulbs erupted the moment he looked down at her and too late, she realized the photo she'd just given them. The romantic embrace they appeared to be in would make front and center of the tabloids' covers. To her surprise, BJ smiled down at her and winked; for a moment, she thought he was going to kiss her. He dipped his chin and then paused and pulled back. Instead of kissing her, he gave her a gentle squeeze and then focused on the crowd.

"If you boys want a story, it's not here. I can assure you that Olivia was blindsided by that kiss from Brad Pearson because she's with me, and I can guarantee you she didn't need a thing from Brad Pearson."

Olivia gasped at his words and then before she had time to get her thoughts together, BJ blindsided her with a kiss of his own.

She wanted to be furious. She really did but at the moment, all she could do was grab hold of him and hang on as cameras snapped and she experienced the kiss of her life.

It was more than the kiss on the boat. This kiss was powerful, overwhelming, and clearly stating to anyone watching that she was his woman.

The tabloids were going to have a field day tomorrow.

But she didn't even care. BJ had basically thrown down the gauntlet and she instinctively wrapped her arms around his neck and held on.

CHAPTER NINE

*H*e had lost his mind, he concluded halfway through kissing Olivia. *This was her reputation and he was acting just like that jerk Pearson.*

Except that he realized he could kiss Olivia for the rest of his life.

But this could hurt her.

Slowly his senses returned and he pulled away, looked down at her and braced for outrage.

Instead, she was smiling. "Well," she whispered, "when you say let's give them something to talk about, you really give them something to talk about."

"This could cause you more problems."

"At this moment, I don't care." She then took him by surprise and pulled his head back to hers and kissed him thoroughly.

"Are you two going to do that all day?" someone yelled.

Olivia chuckled against BJ's lips. "Maybe."

He smiled into the cameras. "If we want to. We are not your entertainment. You can leave whenever you want to."

Olivia giggled and BJ almost busted out laughing at the cameramen's expressions.

He looked down at her. "I could kiss you all day and let them take the same photo over and over again but I'm starved. How about you?"

She nodded. "Let's go inside."

Keeping her close, he pushed through the cameramen. An older man standing beside the doormen waved them toward the open door.

"Horace," Olivia exclaimed. "Thank you."

"Get on in there, little lady. We'll take care of this."

Olivia wanted to give him a hug but decided getting inside was best. This had been a very unexpected turn of events.

"Thanks," BJ told the older man Olivia had called Horace. He nodded curtly, and then practically pushed them through the door, which immediately closed behind them. BJ looked back and several doormen and bellhops moved to stand in front of all the doors. The fiasco was over. At least for the moment.

"Who was that guy?"

"That's Horace Finley. He's been the handyman and the maintenance man here at the resort since I was a little girl. He'll make the guys keep them out of that entrance. But the beach is public, so there is no keeping them from there. So we could have more photo ops." She laughed.

"Well, I promise I won't be kissing you again. I hope I didn't just make life harder on you."

She cocked her head and hit him with wide eyes. "And what if I want you to kiss me again?"

"As much as I enjoy it, I'm worried what those guys are going to plant on the cover of those magazines tomorrow."

"So? I've lost my job. My reputation is already shredded. So what's one more? And this one I actually liked."

"Hey you two," Cali called from the upper level. "That was some show you two put on out there."

"How did you see us?" BJ asked and then it hit him—they had security cameras.

"Smile, you're on *Candid Camera.*" She laughed. "Come up here. Jillian is on the phone to the restaurant, getting you two a table."

"Let the games continue." Olivia chuckled and led the way through the small group in the hotel lobby and up the curving stairs.

"You two were pretty cozy out there. Did you want to set the tabloids on fire tomorrow?" Cali asked the minute they reached her.

"It just happened," Olivia told her older sister.

BJ kept quiet and let the sisters talk. He could only imagine what kind of trouble was going to break out tomorrow when Olivia's brothers and dad saw the magazines. He was fairly certain they would not be smiling about the photos. The sisters seemed to take it in stride and actually seemed thrilled about the situation considering they were arranging dinner. It was baffling.

"We assumed you would want dinner near the beach so we're having our best table prepared. If the cameramen want another photo, they are going to have to work for it."

Jillian was hanging up the phone as they moved inside. "So, Levi briefed us about the plan, so we've been waiting. Now you're all set. He didn't fill us in on the plan to start new rumors, though." Jillian and Olivia looked almost identical…and to most people they were. But BJ knew the twinkle in Olivia's eyes and the way she considered things before she spoke. He knew Olivia by heart. Jillian was beautiful, too, but from the moment he'd met her at the hospital during Gage's emergency surgery, he'd never felt anything for her other than that she was a nice person.

He'd felt instant chemistry with Olivia the

moment he'd touched her hand and looked into her eyes that morning she was stuck on the roof.

"Thank you for doing this, BJ," Jillian said, breaking into his thoughts."

"Glad to," he said. "We knew this is where they'd be camped out. We thought about making them work to find us but decided to be obvious and get it over with."

Cali and Jillian were all smiles.

"Oh, you were obvious." Cali chuckled.

"I hope I haven't made life harder for Olivia by what happened out there."

Jillian and Cali studied Olivia, who looked completely unfazed.

"She looks okay to me," Cali chirped.

"Me too," Jillian agreed. "Now go. The evening is young and romance is in the air at Windswept Bay."

He wasn't exactly sure what to say to that and didn't have time to anyway as Cali held open a door at the back of the room, and Olivia took his arm and led him out onto a stairwell on the outside of the building.

Somehow he sensed that he'd lost control of the evening after all. But he was more than ready to find some time alone with her.

The sun was hanging just above the water as they walked up the charming plank bridge that led to the lovely outdoor restaurant that overlooked the beach and the water. The candlelit tables on the deck were quiet and very romantic. Olivia's stomach fluttered as she envisioned finally sitting down with BJ for, at least, a partial bit of privacy.

Their hostess was Blair, a nice girl who Olivia didn't know. She led them to a table in the corner of the deck. There was a large planter cutting the table off from all the others.

BJ paused at it. "Is that always here?"

"Honestly, it's been awhile since I was here but I have a sneaking suspicion that it appeared moments ago per instructions from the main office."

"I thought it was in an odd position. But I'm glad

to see it. Your sisters seem to be enjoying this evening almost as much as I am." BJ chuckled and held Olivia's chair for her as she sat.

"I think you're right." Olivia smiled at the hostess as she accepted a menu from her. "Thank you for this arrangement."

"Oh, you're welcome. And if you notice, the rocks there," she pointed out toward the beach and the rocky area, "makes it hard on snoopy people to be snoopy."

BJ laughed. "Well, look at that. They'll have to work hard if they want a shot of this dinner."

"Yes, sir, that is the plan."

"Your sisters have a wicked sense of humor. I like it."

Olivia looked around. "I wonder if they are hunkered down somewhere, waiting to see if any cameramen get doused out there when the tide rushes in."

BJ looked startled. "You mean they're going to get out there and then get wet?"

"Oh, not too bad. Just a little if they don't leave

before it gets dark."

"Well, as long as it's not dangerous and we don't have to go out there and rescue someone then I guess we're okay. The last thing we need is to be in the news for endangering someone."

Olivia patted his arm. "Stop worrying. They are big boys and they do not have to get on the rocks. Especially since there are signs everywhere telling them to stay off the rocks. They've gotten enough photos. They've gotten quotes. They have what they need so they can go home now." And Olivia meant it. She was tired of them. What she wanted was to have this evening with BJ without distractions.

BJ covered her hand with his. "I have enjoyed every moment of this unexpected day. And I assure you, if you need to do more kissing for the camera, I will do it. I am your man, Olivia Sinclair."

Her skin tingled with awareness and Olivia's heart thundered at his words. She struggled not to wear her heart in her expression. "But you said there would be no more kissing," she said, breathlessly.

He sighed. "A man will do what he needs to do. So if the need arises, I'm all in."

How could this man make her smile with every fiber of her being? "I hope it does."

"So do I."

Maybe she didn't want the paparazzi to go away just yet after all.

CHAPTER TEN

Olivia woke the next morning smiling.

She was up early and had a cup of coffee while she sat on the deck, enjoying the sunrise and thoughts of the wonderful day before.

Dinner had been amazing, though she could have eaten cardboard and she wouldn't have known it. BJ was mesmerizing. They'd quickly been lost in conversation and had actually forgotten about the cameras that might or might not be snapping their photo. They hadn't even paid attention to whether anyone dared to climb out onto the rocks and risked getting caught in the tide.

She'd asked him once again about his feelings about having just found out that he had a brother he'd never known. And she'd instantly known that she'd hit a chord.

He'd tensed. "It's hard realizing you have a family you were kept from. I have a sense of betrayal that I don't like thinking about where my mother is concerned. Then again, I also wonder, why did she take me and run? But not just run—she hid me. Why?"

Olivia wondered that too.

Maybe the lawyer would have the answers BJ needed.

He and Lilly had followed their dreams after losing their parents but Olivia could tell he missed his sister. Olivia hoped she would come to Windswept Bay at some point.

She also hoped that in two days when Gage and Shar arrived home from their honeymoon that the two brothers could begin the process of bonding.

Olivia was ready to spend some quality time with her parents and siblings too, she realized. Time that didn't involve paparazzi. BJ's situation gave her a new perspective on her own family and she was glad she was home. Finishing her coffee, she stood and headed inside. It was time to get dressed. She was going to spend time with her family while she tried to figure out what she was going to do with her life after all the scandal blew over.

BJ had gone out early for some quiet time on the early morning ocean. It was a favorite time of day for him, especially when he needed to think.

Soon he was going to need to start booking some fishing charters to replenish his bank account. But not yet. There was so much going on in his life, he'd needed the time.

The fact that he had inherited a fortune still seemed unreal and he couldn't even bring himself to embrace the idea. Even almost two weeks after having learned who he was.

He made a good living with his fishing charters. Certainly nothing in the realm of wealth but he had a life most people would envy and everything he could want. And he had the freedom to go wherever and whenever he wanted. That was priceless.

To know now that he had more than he would ever need or use in his lifetime was unsettling. He needed to talk to the lawyer. Tomorrow would be here soon enough, he told himself. But he was ready. It was time to get this all sorted out because he had more important things to focus on than money and even an inheritance. He had Olivia to focus on.

She was amazing and he couldn't get her off his mind. She was there constantly. Everything else was squeezed into a side pocket of his thoughts while she filled everything else with her wit and charm and lovely self.

And she was lovely.

If he could have her, he'd give everything else up, even his boat and his lifestyle. He hadn't gone to bed after dropping her off at her place after an amazing three-hour dinner that had been spent talking about everything and anything. And mixed with so much laughter that he'd needed.

And he knew he would do what it took to see whether the two of them stood a chance of having more together after both of their lives settled down and they regained their equilibrium.

There was no doubt that he was falling for her.

He docked the boat around eight and was securing it to the pier when he glanced toward Shar's place, hoping to glimpse Olivia on the deck having coffee. What he saw chilled him to the bone.

A man was half hidden in the trees, watching the back deck. If it hadn't been for his red shirt, BJ might not have spotted him. *What kind of professional snooper wore a red shirt when hiding in bushes?* BJ didn't wait to find out the answer. He took off running across the sand, hoping to make it to the tree line before the man turned and spotted him.

Obviously he hadn't heard him drive in with the boat and BJ figured that might have been a little helping hand from the man upstairs.

When he reached the trees, he moved quietly and slowly as he made his way through the bushes to where he was within only ten or so feet from the jerk.

"Hands in the air and don't run or I'll shoot," he growled, bluffing as he didn't have a weapon on him.

The man froze and dropped his huge camera. "Don't shoot," he said. "I'm unarmed." Lucky for him, his camera was attached to a strap around his neck and had been saved from hitting the ground.

BJ felt no sympathy either way. He figured the photos on the camera could be used as evidence if they needed it.

"You're a trespasser, spying on my friend," BJ corrected him.

"No, I'm on the beach. It's not private property."

"From where I'm standing, that's more grass than sand under your feet." BJ pulled out his phone. "I'm calling this in. You just stay put."

"No need. I'm here." Levi came from around the corner of the bungalow. He did not look happy. He hadn't shaven and his eyes were dark slits as he pulled cuffs from his waistband.

"You are on private property and caught on surveillance cameras from several different angles. You're about to spend time in my jailhouse. You and your buddies have prevented me from getting my beauty rest and you know what happens when I don't get my rest? I get grumpy and have no sense of humor or forgiveness. That means everyone goes to jail. No second chances."

"Come on, man. I need to get paid too, you know. I'm just doing my job."

Levi grabbed him by the arm, spun him around and snapped the cuffs in place. "You should have thought about that before you started snooping. You need a new occupation. Because in my jurisdiction, being a Peeping Tom is against the law."

"I'm no Peeping Tom—"

"Zip it, man. You're already on my bad side."

"You got it from here, I assume?" BJ asked.

"I've got it. That and a headache." He shot BJ a scowl. "Thanks for looking out for Olivia."

"Glad to do it."

"We'll talk about that kiss later," Levi shot back.

"What?"

"Yeah, the tabloids are out and you and my sister are all over it. 'The Kiss That Wouldn't Stop' was one headline."

"Oh, *that* kiss." BJ smiled.

"Yeah. Is that what you call looking out for her?"

"Actually, yes. But, I understand if you're upset. Believe me, my intentions are honorable."

Levi hitched a brow at BJ and then nudged the grumbling cameraman forward. "I don't know if you've noticed but my sister is a fully grown, independent woman very capable of figuring her life out all by herself. The only reason I butted in on the paparazzi is because this was about stalking, in my eyes. And not her choice. For what it's worth, I think the two of you are a good fit. Tell her I said she needs to close her blinds." And then Levi led the bewildered photographer around the corner of the house and out of sight.

BJ stared after them for a moment and then headed to the back deck and went to knock on the door. It swung open before he knocked.

"I just got off the phone with Levi's dispatcher. Did you get him?"

"He's headed to the jailhouse with your brother."

"Good. Where did you come from?"

"The boat dock. I spotted him from there and snuck up on him."

"And I missed it. I bet you scared him to death."

"Did you ever stop and think he might have been dangerous?" BJ asked, his temper flaring suddenly.

"He had a big camera with a massive wide angled zoom on it. Did you get a look at that thing?"

"Okay, so you're right about that. I thought it was going to knock the breath out of him when he dropped it and it slammed him in the chest." He smiled at her and pulled her into his arms. "Does trouble follow you around like this all the time?"

"No. I'm usually pretty boring. I know it's hard to believe but it's true. Really."

"I'll believe that when I see it. So far my experience with you has been a rooftop escapade and days of paparazzi. I'm just having fun waiting for the next exciting installment of the *Olivia Sinclair Reality Show*."

She scowled. "Funny."

"Entertaining."

She shook her head. "Well, today I won't be your entertainment. I'm sneaking off for a secret rendezvous with my mother and dad. We gave the media a story and now I'm going off grid for a few days. Hopefully they'll be gone by the time I show back up in two days."

"You're leaving?"

"My parents are meeting me in Naples for a couple of days. If I'm lucky, by the time we get back, everyone will have gotten bored hanging out and be gone and when Gage and Shar arrive home, all will be back to normal in Windswept Bay."

"How are you getting to Naples? Do you need me to take you?"

"You went above and beyond the call of duty yesterday and I appreciate it very much. But today I'm giving you the day off. Jake is coming by to get me. He's driving me down to Naples. Besides that, you have to get ready for your big outing tomorrow with the lawyer. Relax. Jake can take care of me too. I see the worry in your eyes."

It was true. But he had to agree with that—Jake

looked as if he could handle himself very well. From what he had gathered, Jake had been something in the military and now owned a dive shop. BJ knew Olivia was in good hands.

He just wasn't ready to let go of her himself.

"Okay, Jake will take care of you," he agreed and then kissed her forehead. And he did need to get ready for tomorrow.

"Are you still worried about what the lawyer has to say?"

"I'm still conflicted," he admitted. "But contrary to what you might think, I spent very little time worrying about that last night. I had my mind on something, or someone else." He fought the urge to kiss her.

Olivia's eyes turned misty green. "I think maybe what is going on between us is moving a little fast."

She wasn't denying it, he realized. Just acknowledging it.

"I can handle slowing down," he said, without hesitation. "Whatever it takes."

"I think we're in agreement then. I'll go with my

mom and dad, spend a little quality time with them and give you time to sort through what you learn tomorrow."

He nodded slowly and then he took her face gently in his hands. His heart faltered, as if stumbling over itself when her gaze held his. "You mesmerize me, Olivia." And then he captured her lips with his.

It was a short, but lingering kiss that he ended far sooner than he'd wanted to. "I'm hoping to get more of that next time I see you."

"We're slowing it down." Her eyes twinkled again.

"But not regressing."

She laughed softly. "We'll see," she teased.

His heart melted.

CHAPTER ELEVEN

"You were right," Larry Stewart said proudly the next day as he held up a nice-sized bluefin tuna. "This should have been on my bucket list a long time ago. I'm hooked." He chuckled at his play on words.

The lawyer was in his seventies and had a dignified way about him that caused BJ to immediately think the man would find deep sea fishing appalling. He hadn't; he'd loved it and it had, so far, been a great day to fish.

"You're really good at being a captain," Larry

observed as BJ took the tuna and put it in the ice chest with the other fish that Larry had caught so far. "Your father would have been proud of you."

BJ had his back to Larry when he made the statement and the words hit him like a cold blast. Turning around, he met Larry's thoughtful gaze. "Tell me about Milton Lancaster. I know very little about him. Gage and I have had very little time together to discuss any of this. Like I explained on the phone the other day, I've basically learned my life wasn't exactly what I was led to believe. It's a jolt to learn I have a father other than the man I called father and loved and respected. To be fair to Milton, I know that he has spent a lot of money over the years looking for me after my mother took me and disappeared. It still makes hearing that he's my dad and would be proud of me a little disconcerting."

Larry sat down in the seat and looked solemn. "I understand. I knew Milton most of his adult life. We met right out of college, so I can assure you he was a good man. He was a man who experienced a lot of early loss when he lost his first wife in childbirth and was left with a baby son and absolutely no idea how to raise the boy. Gage was raised by nannies until the age of ten, when his father then started taking him to work with him. It was what Gage wanted and in his own way, it made Milton happy to have his son beside him. But Milton worked too hard, put too much of himself into his work and building his wealth portfolio than he spent developing a meaningful relationship with his son. But he loved Gage. And Gage never knew exactly what drove his dad to be the man that he was. I advised him many times to tell Gage about you, but I was his legal counsel and by that, my hands were tied. But losing you when you were a baby sent Milton into a tailspin that he never fully recovered from."

It was surreal hearing about the man he was supposed to have feelings for. He felt more for Gage and the way he was brought up. True, he'd had everything a kid could want in the way of food, a safe place to live, and the best of care. But unlike the happy, carefree childhood that BJ had experienced, Gage had missed out on a normal way of life. And Larry was telling BJ that it was his fault. "I still don't get it. This is all very hard to take in."

The boat rocked gently on the waves as BJ moved to sit in his seat.

Larry nodded agreement. "Bear with me. Your father had lost his first wife, whom he adored, and he was grief-stricken. And then, nearly a year later, he was down here looking at a business he was buying when he met a woman on the beach early one morning when he was out jogging. He fell for your mother hard. It surprised him and changed him. And that year he spent much time here in Windswept Bay. Gage was still a small child and he was well taken care of back in New York. When Milton learned your mother was pregnant, he was ecstatic. He called me immediately and told me the news. And altered his will that day to include you. He had plans to marry your mother and unite his family as one.

"I had never seen him happier. But your mother, whom I will admit I had never met, loved her life in Florida and had a huge aversion to moving to the city. Much like you." He smiled. "By the time you were a toddler, he wanted to combine his family but they fought bitterly over her not wanting to move. He needed to be, or so he thought, in New York in order to really build the business that he wanted. And as you can gather, it wasn't long after that that your mother took you and went away. And Milton became emotionally distant after that. It was like a light went off in him. Work became his priority after that. But he never gave up hope of finding you. And your mother. He didn't talk of it often, but when he did, it was obvious how painful it was for him."

"Why did my mother run? The question keeps roaming through my mind." BJ could feel for Milton, but he still didn't understand.

"Milton told me he made the mistake of telling your mother that he would fight for custody. And not long after that, she disappeared.

"He regretted his words for the rest of his life. For all of you."

BJ was silent. There was nothing to say as he let all of it sink in. It was a hard situation. But he still felt nothing for Milton other than a sense of regret for the man. BJ's mother had done what she must have believed was her only option. She hadn't wanted to live in the city…and yet she'd obviously fallen for Milton; it was clear in the photos they loved each other. They'd just wanted different things out of life and had different visions for raising their son.

"For what it's worth, your father never stopped loving you or believing he would find you. He kept the house here all these years because of your mother. He never stopped loving her either. Are you ready to go over the will? I have a copy of it in my briefcase."

BJ stared out over the blue calm water as his insides churned as though a storm had swept into the bay. "No, Larry, I think I want to fish for a while. How about you?"

Larry grinned. "I'm in agreement. It's just money and property being discussed in there. I just told you the important information. You and Gage will have to navigate your way from here on out. I'll advise you all you want but I think the most important thing in Milton's heart was that the two of his boys would become brothers."

"I'll be glad when Gage arrives home sometime

tomorrow. We have a lot to go over together and decisions to be made…and yes, we need to get to know each other. He's a good guy. I've already figured that out and I haven't even been around him that much."

Larry crossed his arms and studied him. "Something tells me, though, that all of this means very little to you."

"I just don't know how to wrap my head around this newfound wealth. Like I told you on the phone, I'm happy with my life. Content. And that's something a lot of people don't understand."

Larry moved to pick up his fishing rod. "I'm beginning to. I think you're going to have to put me down as a regular charter from here on out. Believe me, if you can learn to navigate these waters, you'll learn to navigate the new path of your life. It will only change you if you want it to."

BJ chuckled. Larry was alright. "You have a point there, Larry."

"Now, are you ever going to mention why I saw photos of you kissing that lovely young woman splashed all across the newsstands in the airport?"

BJ laughed at the unexpected question. His thoughts went to Olivia. He hoped she was having a good time with her parents. She, too, was learning to navigate uncharted waters.

"Well, Larry, do you have time for a long story?"

"I have all day. And something tells me this is going to be a good story."

BJ's heart warmed, thinking of Olivia. "You're right about that. Absolutely the best story."

The moment Olivia and her parents arrived back in town, her sisters met them at Shar's house to prepare for the coming home party that they were throwing for them that evening. Their plane was due to arrive at St. Pete-Clearwater International Airport around four and they wanted to have everything ready.

To Olivia's relief, Levi had informed them yesterday that it seemed all of her "admirers" had grown bored and gone back to the land of the stars. He'd also had her take a look at the new tabloid. It seemed that Brad Pearson had gotten himself into a bit of trouble—which came to no surprise to Olivia. Someone had finally figured out that the second photo that everyone had claimed was her and Brad was not Olivia. And they'd caught him with the wife of one of the higher-up executives of the studio he was contracted with.

And in that one moment, Olivia understood why he'd kissed her. She just happened to resemble in size and coloring the woman he was really seeing. So Olivia had been a decoy.

"So," Jillian said as she walked through the door of Shar's home. "How does it feel to be scandal-free?"

"For a decoy, I think she held up really well." Cali gave her a hug.

Violet, their mother, pushed a thick strand of charcoal grey hair behind her ear and frowned. "The lack of class that man showed is shocking. To use Olivia like that is just appalling. And she lost her job."

"Mom, wow," Olivia said, shocked by her normally calm mother's outburst. Cali and Jillian looked just as startled. "I love you, too. And I'm okay. Really, I am. Despite everything that went on in my life in the last two weeks, back in Hollywood and then followed me here…" She smiled. "I've actually had one of the best weeks of my life."

All eyes were on her.

Cali didn't look surprised at all. "Does that have something to do with your sister's new brother-in-law?"

Olivia nodded. Her heart swelled just thinking about BJ. "It does. He's so kind. And amazing."

"And," Jillian added with a smile, "he's obviously a great kisser from the now famous tabloid cover."

Violet's expression softened. "You're in love. I knew you had something on your mind these last two days and with all the humming you were doing, it didn't seem to be anything horrible."

Olivia took a deep breath. *Was she in love?* "I know I've never felt this way before. But BJ has a lot on his plate right now. His entire world has been turned upside down, and so I'm just content to be here for him as he figures things out. We've just met but this last week had a lot packed into it and it seems like I've known him much longer."

"You two were inseparable for about three days there," Cali pointed out.

Three wonderful days, Olivia agreed but kept the thought to herself.

She couldn't wait to see BJ and find out how his time with the lawyer had gone.

"Speaking of BJ, I think I better call him and let him in on our impromptu plans for this party and make sure we can come down and hijack the house since he's been staying there. I'll just step outside."

She left her family as they busied themselves with the food preparations for the party. Olivia walked out onto the deck and pulled out her phone. She glanced down the beach toward the dock and her heart caught in her chest at the sight of BJ working on his boat. He had his shirt off and even from this distance, she could see his tanned muscles gleaming in the sunlight.

She saw him reach to his left and pick up the phone. He looked toward Shar's place as he answered.

"You're back." He waved from the boat. "What are you doing up there? Come on over, pretty lady."

She laughed. "Hello to you too."

"Hello," he said, gruffly. "I've missed you."

Three simple words meant so much. "I've missed you, too."

"Then why are we talking on the phone?" he asked and she watched as he hopped from the boat to the dock and strode to the sand.

Olivia moved from the deck and onto the sandy path and made her way to the beach. "Meet you halfway." She ended the call and then dropped the phone in her pocket and started to jog. It was hard to do in her flip-flops, so she kicked them off and kept on jogging. Her sundress swirled around her thighs and before she had gotten too far, she had to grab the skirt and hold it as she jogged to keep the breeze from hiking it to her waist.

BJ was laughing when he reached her. "Having trouble there?" In one quick motion, he swept her into his arms and kissed her.

Olivia knew in that moment that nothing in her life was ever going to be the same. She was most certainly in love with BJ. And she hoped he felt the same way.

BJ had to make himself bring the kiss to a halt and then he just held Olivia in his arms, feeling her heartbeat against his. Ever since he'd learned that his life was not what he'd always believed, he'd felt a bit as if he were fluttering in the wind like her cute dress had been before he'd helped her out by scooping her into his arms. Olivia did that for him. When she was near, he felt grounded again. He didn't know where he was going with everything else in his life but he knew what he hoped for when he looked at Olivia.

A lifetime.

Forever.

"So did you have a good two days with your parents?"

"I did. Not a photographer lurking in the bushes anywhere trying to get a picture. It was heavenly."

He laughed, feeling the rumble of pure satisfaction in his chest. "And they're not here anymore either. Just like you'd predicted."

"I know. I hear they're back in Hollywood, trying to get the new scoop on bad Brad."

"So I hear. So how does it feel to have been a pawn in his sinister scheme?"

Her smile broadened and she rested a hand against his cheek. "I hope you don't mind me saying this, but it brought me home and I met you, so all is wonderful. I have no complaints."

"That's what I wanted to hear." He kissed her neck and breathed in the soft scent of her. "You know you drive me crazy?"

She smiled. "I hope so. If not, I'd be very disappointed."

He lifted his head with the intention of kissing her again when he spotted three people on the deck of Shar's house. "Are those your sisters?"

Olivia gasped. "Yes, I forgot." She giggled. "You distracted me. That is Cali and Jillian and my mom. We are giving a surprise welcome home party to Shar and Gage. And since they will be moving into the big house for a while, do you mind if we come over and decorate?"

"Not at all. I've already washed my sheets and moved back to the boat. I'm getting it ready to start charters next week."

"Oh, but you own part of the house. I'm sure they don't want you to move out."

"I talked to Gage and insisted that I was just there temporarily. And believe me, I never had any plans to move into that house, especially with a pair of newlyweds. If I ever buy a home, it will be one I pick out and buy."

"I get that."

"Don't get me wrong—I appreciate the offer. But another reality is Gage and I are strangers. Besides everything else that's wrong with me being in the house, the truth is that we need time to get to know each other. Becoming roommates with my new brother isn't on my radar. If I become a roommate with anyone in the future, it will be a very personal choice." He kissed her forehead. "Yes, you girls go take over the house. I am perfectly fine with it."

He set her feet on the ground and she grabbed her

skirt and held it in place. "You are invited. I hope you'll come. We are gathering at four thirty."

"I'll be there. Do you need any help now?"

"No, we've got it." She kissed his cheek. "Are you okay? Did your meeting give you answers?"

"Some. And despite what I just said, I'm looking forward to Gage and Shar arriving home. It will be good to talk to him."

BJ watched Olivia head back to Shar's place and then turned and went back to his boat. Three weeks ago when he'd first docked in Windswept Bay, he hadn't had a clue what was in store for him. He shot a glance over his shoulder at Olivia and saw her disappear inside with her family. He'd tried to call Lilly earlier, needing to hear her voice. It had been weeks since she checked in with him and he at least liked to know she was okay. His sister was a free spirit who liked to do her own thing but still, this was too long. Maybe it was the fact that Olivia had such a large family that had him realizing that he and Lilly needed to connect more. He also needed to tell her about what was going on in his life.

Her phone went straight to voicemail, like it had the last time he'd tried to call. "Lilly, it's me. Call me back, okay? We need to talk… Love you. And Lilly…I miss you." They didn't normally take the time to leave a message. They knew to call back when they saw each other's number so wasting time leaving a message didn't make sense.

When he reached his boat, he checked his watch and realized he only had three hours before the party. He decided he might as well stay docked here until then and then he'd move the boat back to the spot he was leasing at the marina. If he was going to stick around Windswept Bay, and he had plans to do so, then he was going to have to get a truck. He and Olivia had used Shar's Jeep for their date the other night but the next time he took Olivia out, he planned to do it with his own transportation.

CHAPTER TWELVE

"Surprise!"

The crowd of family all shouted with happiness as Gage pulled his car into the driveway amid all the family vehicles. There was no way to hide all of them, so a semi-surprise had been all Olivia and her family could come up with. Despite the fact that it was broad daylight and the yard was full of family, the newlyweds appeared surprised.

Shar was out of the car like a rocket, a huge smile plastered across her face. "Oh, it's so good to see everyone!" She rushed around and gave each family member a hard hug.

Olivia couldn't help the bubble of joy she felt at seeing her dry-witted sister so happy.

"And you," Shar said, when she got to Olivia. "You are here." She engulfed her. "I told Gage that I was going to have to go to Hollywood and kidnap you just to get you home for a visit."

"She did say that," Gage said. "Hello, I'm Gage. It's nice to finally meet you." He was handsome, with a dark hair and eyes that instantly had her attention. They were BJ's eyes. It was unmistakable.

"It's nice to meet you too. I regret so much that I missed your wedding…both times."

Gage's smile widened. "We missed you both times. But you're here now and from what I've been hearing, you have befriended my brother." He held his hand out to BJ, who was standing beside her. "I can't wait to spend time with you at last. We have a lot to talk about."

Olivia liked Gage already and as she looked from BJ to Gage, she saw a new beginning happening in front of her.

"Come on, everyone," Violet called to all of her family. "Let's move this party inside and out on the back deck. We have plenty of food and cold drinks. And Sam has smoked a fantastic brisket for everyone."

"Oh yeah, you're speaking my talk now," Jake called and led the stampede of brothers into the house.

Olivia looked at Shar. "She's laid out a feast in there."

Shar locked arms with her and they headed inside. "She shows her love with food."

Olivia locked arms with her triplet. "I have missed you, sis. But I think I'm going to stick around for a while and see what kind of job turns up for me around here," she said as they entered the house.

Shar stopped. "Are you kidding me? You can have my spot at the resort. Really, you're the PR person. Ask Cali and Jillian how my PR skills are. They are awful. Just awful. It's a wonder I haven't run entire groups off with my mouth. Cali, Jillian—get over here."

Olivia felt a little overwhelmed but then this was Shar and it did not surprise Olivia in the least that her blunt-talking, not-always-filtered sister was not the most diplomatic when it came to public relations.

"Olivia is looking for a job. Did you two know this?"

Cali stared at Olivia, as did Jillian. "You've decided to stay?"

"I think I'd like to. I've really thought about it and I know now that I didn't leave Hollywood, running from scandal. I was running from Hollywood itself. I tried to love it but I just don't."

Jillian hugged her. "Welcome home, sis. And maybe BJ has a little something to do with this?"

Olivia smiled. "Maybe."

"Great." Shar hitched a brow at Cali. "Put her in my job. Now. I'll go work with the sea turtle hospital full-time. With Olivia on board at the resort with you and Jillian, the sky is the limit."

Cali laughed. "Shar is serious, Olivia. If you haven't figured it out. She has tried so hard and we have loved having her but her heart is with saving the sea turtles she loves. And that's where she should be, even if you don't want to step in and take her place.

But we would love to have you join us."

Jillian had been nodding while Cali spoke. "Oh, Olivia, it would be perfect with you there. It would be wonderful for all four of us to be working together but Shar is our Superwoman and we need her to represent us in saving the turtles." Jillian winked at Shar.

Olivia felt tears well in her eyes. "I really would love to join you at the resort. It sounds fabulous."

"Yes!" Shar yelped. "Thank you, God." She looked at the ceiling. "Seriously, thank you, thank you."

"Group hug," Cali said, as she always had when they were kids. And all of them gathered up and hugged.

And Olivia could not believe it had taken her so long to find her way home.

The sun had set when the welcome home party ended and everyone had gone home. Olivia had caught a ride to Shar's place with Jillian, despite him telling her he would walk her home on the beach. She'd told him he needed to spend some time with Gage, and she was right. But this was Gage's first night home from his honeymoon in his house with his bride. BJ was not feeling comfortable about keeping the newlyweds apart but the minute he started to leave, Shar stopped him.

"Hold on there," she demanded from the kitchen, where she was placing the last slice of chocolate cake on a paper plate.

There had been threats to her brothers earlier that no one was to eat her last piece of cake. BJ had thought that the slice of cake would go missing during the good-bye hugs as the brothers had headed out but miraculously it was still sitting on the cake plate.

"Do not walk out that door. Gage is coming in with my suitcase and then you two are going to spend some time together. You're going to take this piece of cake back to the boat with you when you go, too."

He eyed the cake. "Me? That's your cake."

She laughed. "No, I saved it for you. It's your 'I'm glad you're a part of the family' slice." She covered it with foil, walked around the counter and into the living room area, and held it out to him. "Welcome to the family, BJ."

BJ took the cake. "Thanks. You know that if your brothers learn I got this piece of cake, they might hurt me."

She laughed. "You look like you can hold your own. But if you don't want it, I can keep it." She started to take it back but he held on and grinned.

"I think I'll risk it."

"Risk what?" Gage walked into the kitchen with two large suitcases.

"Her brothers' wrath when they find out your wife gave me the last piece of chocolate cake."

"Hey, I thought that was for me?"

Shar walked into the kitchen and picked up two plastic forks; she came back and handed them both one.

"You can share it. Now, go. My head hurts thinking about all the stuff you have to discuss. Besides being newfound brothers, you own this gosh awful gigantic corporation together. I've hogged Gage long enough. Have at it, boys. And enjoy the cake."

With that, she strode out of the room and headed up the stairs.

Gage was all smiles as he watched her go. "Man, I love her. That is some kind of woman."

BJ thought of Olivia. He hadn't been able to keep his eyes off her all evening. "You two look really happy."

Gage nodded. "I don't know what I did to deserve her but I'm grateful. Come on. Show me your boat. And bring that cake."

They walked down the short path and across the sand to the pier. The light from the windows of the captain's quarters helped illuminate the boat deck as they went on board. "You're getting around good," he said. "Has the gunshot wound completely healed?"

"I still feel a twinge every now and again. But mostly it's healed."

"Glad to hear it." He took the wrapper off the cake and set it on the table on the deck. They both stared at it and then, laughing, they sat down and each dug their fork into it.

"So…" Gage paused before he stuffed his fork

into his mouth.

BJ didn't hesitate; he had the cake in his mouth almost instantly and was chewing when Gage dropped his bombshell.

"Do you want to buy me out of my share of the business?"

BJ choked. "What?" he wheezed.

Gage reached over and slapped him on the back. "Sorry, man—didn't mean to do that to you."

After a moment, BJ got his breath back and stared at his brother. "You want me to buy you out? I don't want your business. I was going to make you the same offer. I was actually going to walk away completely, but Larry told me there were provisions that didn't allow me to walk away. That everything would remain in my name and that wouldn't be fair leaving you to run the corporation alone while I reaped the benefits. So I was going to sell it to you at a rock-bottom price."

Gage shook his head and finally bit into the cake. "Our dad, if you haven't figured it out, was a brilliant man in business. But he was unlucky in love. I've given this a lot of thought. He worked all the time and he had a silent pain that I never knew about while he lived. And that was you. As a kid, I had everything I could want except time with my dad. He barely spent time at home because he pretty much lived at the office. And when he wasn't at the office, he was on business trips."

Gage laid his fork down, stood up and walked to the boat railing. "Do you know what it was like when I found those pictures of him on this beach, playing and laughing with you when you were a toddler? It was like my heart was ripped out of my chest." His voice was raspy with emotion. "Sorry, man," Gage continued after he cleared his throat. "You had everything I longed for as a kid but you were a toddler and probably have no memory of anything in those photos."

"I don't," BJ said. "But I'm sorry you didn't have that. I had it with my dad. The dad that I know."

They stared at each other.

"It's messed up." Gage laughed gruffly.

"Yeah, it is," BJ agreed. "I don't understand it at all. My mother looked about as in love in those pictures as any woman could be. And I have to admit that I never saw that kind of look in her eyes with my dad. She was happy and loved her life but when I saw those photos, it was the look of love in her expression when she looked at your dad that got me in the gut. I didn't know who the kid was but I knew who she was."

"And that's the million-dollar question then: why did she leave and break my dad's heart? Because I'm convinced that's what happened. He lost my mom, then found your mom, and then he lost her and you when she ran away. Me, I lost him and my mom the day I was born…at least the dad I longed for. When I was ten and had run the latest nanny off, he started taking me to the office with him and I found a new family in the people who worked in the office. And as I grew, I learned the business and the more I learned, the more time I got to spend with Dad."

He paused. "Shar helped me figure this out while we were gone. He'd lost so much that he couldn't get close anymore. Only through what he did best and always succeeded at and that was business. This business is his way of showing us his love. He never stopped hoping he would find you. And he provided for you from the day you were conceived."

It still made BJ uncomfortable and sad. "Part of me wishes I'd known him but in wishing that, I might never have known *my* dad. I might not ever know why my mom left. But all I can think of is what Larry said, that they fought over him wanting her to move to New York and she refused. I think that has to be it, that she was afraid your dad, our dad, would try to gain custody of me and he was the one with the money."

"That's what I think too. It's the only thing that fits."

"So where does that leave us?" BJ asked. "Because if you think my mom had an aversion to the big city, believe me, it could not compare to what I feel for it. Out there is where I was born to be." He looked out at the moonlit water. "Not holed up in a skyscraper, making money I'll never be able to spend in my lifetime."

"Then, we both sell. I can have buyers lined up tomorrow. We sell and make the lives we want." Gage held out his hand.

BJ stood. "Deal." And they clasped hands and shook.

"Something tells me this is right. This house, this beach. This, I believe, is where he was happiest. And that's why he never sold it."

BJ's heart tugged thinking about the man he'd never know. "I think you're probably right."

CHAPTER THIRTEEN

Olivia went to the resort the next day. She'd sat on her deck for a long time last night, watching BJ and Gage talk on the boat. And then, feeling guilty for watching them even from the distance, she'd gone inside and gone to bed. She hoped things had gone well. BJ's boat had been gone when she woke up.

On the way to the resort, she paused as she drove Shar's Jeep past the marina and scanned the boats docked there but didn't see him. She tried to tell herself not to be nervous. That he hadn't left. But there was a small part of her that feared exactly that. *Would*

BJ stay in Windswept Bay?

"Yes, he will," she chided herself as she drove on to the resort. She had hopes that what they'd shared over the last week had been as special to him as it was to her. He acted like it. His kisses, his gentleness with her, the way he looked at her. It all told her in her heart that he had fallen for her as much as she'd fallen for him.

It was too soon to be spouting words of love. It was time to let their relationship develop.

She just needed to relax and let things continue to develop.

Horace was changing out a wall socket when she entered the lobby and immediately she went over to him. "Horace, I am so glad to see you and be able to tell you thank you for helping out the other evening."

"Olivia, I've been hoping you'd come by now that those vultures are gone. It is really nice to have you back home."

"I'm glad too. Did you hear the news that I'm coming on board with Cali and Jillian here at the resort?"

He looked over his glasses. "I heard. And Superwoman is free to fly."

Olivia smiled at the nickname. "Yes, she is. Her love for the sea turtles and helping grow the hospital and the efforts along the coast is just where she needs to be. And now she has Gage to partner with. It's going to be perfect for her, and for me."

"Good. You gals are making your parents proud. The resort is doing good, looking good, and when they finally get the rooms remodeled, it's going to be classier than it's ever been."

"That's due to Shar, Jillian, and Cali. I hope I can add something to what they've done."

"You will. No doubt in my mind."

"Thanks. See you later."

"I'm always hanging out somewhere."

Olivia smiled at everyone she passed and noticed many of the workers do a double take as she passed by. Being Jillian's identical twin was going to cause a few humorous moments... It hit her suddenly that BJ had never gotten her and Jillian mixed up except the first time they met on the roof and he'd thought she was Jillian. After that, he'd never confused them again.

Not that they had been together all that much when BJ had been around but still somehow she felt he knew who she was no matter what. *Why or how did he know?*

It was a question she planned to ask him.

She entered the office smiling. "I'm reporting for duty." She loved the startled look on Cali's face. "What, you didn't expect me? And you weren't watching the surveillance cameras?"

Cali jumped up and rushed forward. "I'm thrilled you're here. I just didn't expect you to start right after we talked about it."

Olivia set her purse down. "Cali, I have had about all the downtime I can tolerate. And truthfully, if I continue to have nothing to do, I'm afraid I'm going to start stalking BJ and looking needy."

Cali put her hands to her cheeks and laughed.

"I heard that." Jillian chuckled as she came through the door behind Olivia. She was in jeans with a big work shirt and dirt clung to her knees. She carried a potted plant; she set it on the desk and turned to Olivia with a huge smile. "Ignore my attire—it's gardening day. You look lovely and not needy at all and I have a very good feeling that BJ would not object to you being in his life twenty-four hours a day. He could not take his eyes off you last night. And even offered to walk you home."

Cali agreed. "And you denied him the privilege and rode with Jillian instead."

"He needed time with Gage."

"True." Jillian plucked a leaf from her sleeve. "But he wanted to spend time with you. We could tell."

"I'm a full-grown, independent, career woman and I'm feeling a little vulnerable where he's concerned."

"There's no need." BJ stepped around the corner. "Sorry, I didn't mean to eavesdrop. I was just looking for you and I found you. Olivia, my world feels steady and right when you're in it. Before I came to Windswept Bay, I was a content man in every way I could think of. Now, the only time I'm content is when you're with me."

He walked up to her and Olivia had to place a hand on the desk beside her to steady the sudden way the room spun. "I feel the same way," she said. "I just wanted to give you space. You helped me out so much last week."

He took her into his arms. "Last night, Gage and I decided to sell Lancaster Industries. We had a long talk about our father and when we finally parted ways and he went back up to the house, all I wanted was to see you. To tell you what we'd discussed. It didn't feel complete without sharing it with you."

"I love you, BJ," she said, unable to contain her feelings any longer.

His expression grew somber. "And I love you. Through no effort or merit of my own, I'm about to become a very wealthy man. That means I can go anywhere I want, live anywhere I want, and I only want to be where you are. That money means nothing to me except that I can do some good in this world with it. But even that thought means nothing to me without you."

Olivia was smiling through tears as BJ went down on one knee.

"Olivia Sinclair, will you please marry me?"

She leaned down and kissed him. "Yes," she whispered against his lips.

BJ rose and took her into his arms, his blue eyes so tender. "This is the best moment of my life." And then he kissed her breathless and lifted his head. "No, that was the best moment of my life." And then he kissed her again.

When he pulled back, Olivia realized they were alone and the doors to the office were closed. "BJ, I can't believe it."

"Believe what? That I love you?"

"No." She looked around. "That I wish there had been at least one paparazzi hanging around to document that special moment when you knelt and asked me to marry you."

He grinned. "That poor dude Levi arrested might

still be at the jailhouse. We could see if he'd take our picture."

Olivia giggled. "Poor guy. I think I'd just rather have you kiss me again…forever."

"Now, *that* I can do. Always." And he lowered his lips to hers to prove it.

Excerpt from

HOLDING OUT FOR LOVE

Windswept Bay, Book Five

CHAPTER ONE

What am I going to do?

Jillian Sinclair blinked away the tears blurring her vision as she knelt in the flowerbed of Windswept Bay Resort, stunned and disbelieving an hour after leaving the doctor's office. Panic clawed at her throat as she rammed a trowel into the dirt, loosening it up just enough for her to plunge her gloved hands into the softened soil. She removed enough soil to make room for one of the many ferns she and her crew were planting as they prepared for the Thanksgiving Day celebration her family always held for the resort visitors and the people of the community.

Thanksgiving...

Jillian squeezed her eyes tight, pausing movement as she struggled to be thankful after learning her hopes and dreams for her future were ticking away by the moment and were very likely already out of her reach.

She struggled to blink away tears that threatened to expose her pain to anyone who might walk up or ask her a question before she got herself composed.

I will not cry. I will not focus on the glass half-empty...

There was so much in her life to be grateful for...she would focus on that.

But the doctor's words throbbed relentlessly, like a migraine in the forefront of her mind... *"Your opportunities for conceiving will diminish substantially in the next couple of years. The endometriosis is too evasive. A total hysterectomy is unavoidable...sooner than later...I'm so sorry, Jillian."*

No more sorry than Jillian. She wanted children.

Wanted to conceive them, feel them kick inside her womb, feel the joy of their amazing life growing inside her...wanted to know the love of her baby's daddy, experience that blessed journey with the love of her life.

But there was no love of her life on the horizon.

The only thing on her horizon right now was this bombshell dropped on her this morning.

How could recent, painful female troubles be so devastating so quickly...so unexpectedly? To realize that being able to conceive a child would not be an option for her if she didn't act soon... Her heart squeezed and she felt lightheaded, breathless. *She needed a husband.*

She needed him now, if her dream of carrying a child herself were to come to fruition.

But there are options.

The thought was true. Not her first choice. Her dream was the traditional happily-ever-after choice that her three sisters were living and enjoying right now...she wanted that too.

Sitting back on her heels, she pushed her hair from

her face with the back of her gardening glove and let her gaze sweep down the sidewalk to where her crew was getting the soil ready in the larger area of the massive planting. It wasn't just for Thanksgiving but also part of the renovation going on in the rooms on this rear wing of the resort overlooking the beautiful bay. It was a busy time for her as she oversaw the landscaping projects and she loved every aspect of keeping the family resort beautiful for the guests who came here for rest, rejuvenation, and celebrations. Keeping the grounds welcoming and enchanting was a joy to her.

But at the moment, she felt no joy herself.

Planting seedlings and watching them grow and bloom into their full potential was rewarding to Jillian. Watching and helping her children grow into their potential…had been her dream. Motherhood had been her dream. A noise on the second floor drew her attention and she saw Abe, their contractor, help move some plywood into one of the rooms being renovated.

What about Abe?

She and Abe had been out a few times—two

times, to be exact. He was a great person. *Could he be her hope?*

She yanked her gloves off and rubbed her temple. He was handsome in a rugged, strong way and a nice guy, but she felt no sparks, no butterflies when she was around him. Jillian *wanted* butterflies.

Her sisters had butterflies in reaction to the loves of their lives. Each had fallen deeply, madly, hopelessly in love in a short period of time. And she was quite certain that butterflies came with the territory. Considering Jillian was the one who had planted hundreds of butterfly bushes in the landscaping that she adored, there was no way on earth that she would settle for anything less than butterflies when it came to falling in love.

Could she settle for less than that for a baby?

In light of the news today, could she hold out for love?

She was happy for her sisters—really, really happy—but her biological clock was ticking just as quickly as Shar, Olivia, and Cali's. *Ha!* Obviously hers was ticking like a time bomb.

"Hey, sis, how's it going?" Shar called, startling Jillian, as she rushed up the sidewalk. Her dark hair and sparkling green eyes were so different from Jillian and Olivia's that it was hard to believe they were triplets. But they were and in every aspect it seemed but reproduction opportunities.

"Great," Jillian lied and plastered a smile on her face, and was relieved that she'd managed to get the tears under control. "What are you up to today?"

Shar beamed. "I'm on a quick mission to see Abe. Gage and I have been working on plans for enlarging the sea turtle hospital with the funds we're donating in his dad's name. I'm here to see when Abe can come over and give us a bid. I'd love to start it before he finishes the resort—if he has time to oversee the two at the same time."

"Oh, that would be good," Jillian said. Shar loved rescuing sea turtles and she'd found a soul mate who shared her passion. She and Gage were perfect together. Made amazingly for each other. Jillian had always called Shar Superwoman because of her dedication and passion for protecting and rescuing sea life and for helping Windswept Bays Sea Turtle Hospital. God had done an amazing job when he created Gage as the perfect partner for her.

Has God created someone for me?

If so, when was he going to show up? Or was she going to have to forget the butterflies and instead, find a good man to father her baby? Abe was a good man.

Shar studied her. "Are you coming to Cali's housewarming?"

Cali's. "Oh," Jillian gasped and sprang from her kneeling position. "I lost track of the time. I need to get home and take a shower and pick up the appetizers I made." She dusted her knees off and was so glad she had prepared the food before she'd lost her mind this morning at the doctor's office.

Shar laughed. "Hey girl, calm down. I'll let them know you're coming. I'll just be here a moment and then I'm heading over. It's all good."

Jillian didn't share Shar's sentiment. All wasn't good at the moment but she was not going to let anyone know she was struggling with bad news. Now wasn't the time. "I'll hurry and see you there."

It was a rushed drive down the beach to her small bungalow on the hillside over one street from the beach, with a glimpse of the ocean from her backyard. Jillian loved the beach but when she went looking for a home, she chose one with room for her flowers and a view rather than direct access to the beach. She threw off her dusty clothes and wound her thick hair into a coil and clipped it up before she jumped into a barely warm shower.

Still breathless an hour later, Jillian parked her car behind a black Dodge in Cali and Grant's drive and breathed a sigh of relief that she wasn't too late. *How could she have forgotten that her sister was holding a special party with her family tonight?* This was a special time for Cali and Grant, her amazing artist husband. They were so very happy and Jillian was happy for them and her other sisters, Shar and Olivia.

Hurrying from the car, and feeling fragmented, she slammed her door and pulled open the hatchback of her small SUV. She pulled out the large, shallow box holding the cake, pie, and appetizers she'd brought. Her four brothers who were here could put away enough food to feed an army, so it took a lot of food—and she did like to bake and cook, so it was nothing for her to go overboard. But several friends were attending the housewarming too, so going a little overboard on preparation was a good thing.

Her hands were full and she had to shift the box to her hip, and held it precariously. Holding her breath and hoping the box held steady, she reached up, grabbed the hatch and pulled downward. The box on her hip shifted.

She gasped and glanced at the Key lime pie and the three-tiered Italian Cream Cake as they slid to one side of the shallow box, shifting the weight. She knew instantly that it was all about to end up on the pavement. She grabbed for it but knew it was too late.

"Oops, I've got it," a man said, diving out of nowhere, his dark head down as both his hands steadied the box on her hip.

Jillian froze as Ryan Locke lifted his gaze to meet her shocked...and horrified...eyes.

Smooth, masculine, and the one man who'd ever caused her heart to ache with young, foolish love. And he was back in town.

The only man ever to rip her heart to shreds and worse, he didn't even know he'd done it.

Jillian froze as she stared at the man she had never forgotten. She couldn't breathe; she couldn't think as all of her words evaporated. She managed his name. "Ryan."

It took all she had to force his name past frozen lips as memories of the last time she saw him flashed in vivid, mortifying color across her memory.

"It's good to see you, Jillian. It's been a long time."

Nowhere *near* long enough. She wished for the ground to open up and swallow her. She couldn't say anything.

As if not noticing she hadn't said anything, he continued. "I hope you don't mind me dropping in on the party? Jax invited me, and I stopped by and saw Levi at the police department and he invited me, too, so I thought I'd come and say hi to your family."

She cleared the two-ton frog out of her throat. "Oh," she croaked. "Of course I wouldn't mind. Why would I mind?" As soon as the question was out there, she cringed. She knew exactly why he would ask such a question because the last time she'd been in the same room with him, she'd been eighteen and thrown herself at him in the most humiliating way. She felt her cheeks flame and knew she was probably the exact same color as her fuchsia dress.

"Oh, that's great that you and Ryan know each other."

Jillian yanked her eyes off Ryan and felt the flutter of butterflies as she stared in dismay at her friend Blair Baines. Blair was smiling widely at her. She worked for Jillian in the landscape department at the resort. She was also in love with Ryan's cousin Jax, who stood beside her.

As of the last few months, Jax had begun working with Grant, traveling with him sometimes to assist Grant as he painted his world-renowned sea life murals. Jax also owned the Lagoon Adventures in town, a recreation business that did a brisk business in Windswept Bay. They were some of the friends she'd expected to be at this party.

Ryan—she hadn't expected in a million years he would be here.

She thought the world of the younger couple and focused on them as she tried to get a grip on her shock at seeing Ryan for the first time in years. "Yes, we...go way back. Ryan is my brother Levi's best friend." She ventured a glance back at him. He was still as handsome as he'd ever been. His dark-chocolate eyes studied her with butterfly-inducing results. This was not the butterflies she'd just been wishing for earlier. *No, never again where he was concerned.* She yanked her gaze away, disturbed that her pulse careened recklessly and the unwanted butterflies delivered disturbing feelings of that same thrill of attraction that she'd felt as an eighteen-year-old when she looked at the man she'd idolized since childhood.

"Oh, I should have realized that." Blair hugged Jax's arm and beamed up at him. "Jax told me that, duh." She laughed.

Jax grinned. "He's going to run my business while I'm gone to Australia to help Grant with his new mural."

Blair looked sad. "I'm going to miss you the two weeks you'll be gone. But, I'm so glad Ryan could come to help out." She looked back at Jillian. "Jax has been a little stressed lately."

"Hey, I'm fine, Blair." Jax kissed her cheek. "You are the one worrying. This is a great thing for our future."

Jillian felt the love as Jax looked into Blair's eyes. Longing for that kind of love swept over her and she pulled her gaze away and met Ryan's eyes.

Memories hit her like ice water. *Oh and how!* She clutched the box of goodies closer—and decided right then that she might have to hide behind the house and eat every last crumb in hopes to help alleviate her stress.

Blair sighed. "I know, sorry."

The sound of worry in Blair's voice grabbed Jillian's attention. She was one of Jillian's favorite people, and adorably and completely in love with Jax, so what was going on?

"You look great," Ryan said, drawing her attention back to him.

She'd chosen to wear a fuchsia-toned sundress with silver sandals instead of her jeans and boots hoping the outfit would distract her family from noticing she wasn't feeling up to par. "Thank you," she muttered. "I normally have dirt on my knees and smears across my cheeks."

He smiled, despite her not having meant it to be funny.

"You look awesome, Jillian," Blair said. "That dress looks gorgeous on you."

This was getting awkward.

"You look very nice and do clean up good," Ryan said, a teasing light in his eyes. He'd always loved to tease and she'd lapped up every delightful time he'd focused that teasing on her and not one of her sisters.

"What can I say? I love dirt." The statement didn't come out teasingly as she'd hoped, but sounded nervous—was dirt all she could talk about? How had her day gone from horrible to worse this quickly?

She'd hoped being around her family would be a welcome distraction from her troubles. And now...she wanted to throw the desserts in the vehicle and run away. It was so adolescent that she was embarrassed but even that couldn't change how she felt.

"You always did love to play in the dirt." Ryan joined in again.

He was studying her, smiling…looking as handsome as he always had and holding her secrets behind those nearly charcoal eyes of his.

Her insides trembled. He had witnessed the most humiliating day of her life and then he'd left. Hadn't even said good-bye.

Jillian held his gaze, felt hers harden despite struggling desperately to appear unaffected. She was falling apart and she knew it. "I, I need to get these inside. Bye." She didn't meet anyone's eyes and didn't wait for anyone to say more; no, she just made a beeline for the side entrance of Cali's house.

Somewhere behind her, she heard her brother Jake holler Ryan's name and knew she'd have a little time to compose herself as her brothers cornered him.

He had, after all, been a friend of all of her

brothers. He'd been like a sixth son to her parents. And best friends with Levi. And the focus of all of her adolescent admiration.

He was nearly seven years older than her, so much of her life she'd been one of the little sisters. The tagalong. When he'd been a senior in high school, she'd been barely in sixth grade. But just starting to really notice boys and Ryan had gone from being her hero to being her first crush. The problem had been that the crush had never gone away and all through junior high and high school, it had only intensified.

On top of that, Ryan had very nearly begun to ignore her just before when she'd gotten into high school. And then he'd gone off to college and she'd suffered in silence, missing him with all her heart. She hadn't understood why he'd stopped teasing her. She'd told herself it was just because he was older and looking forward to his college life. But when he came home and they ran into each other, he was polite and always seemed ready to get away from her as fast as he could…

Until that night when her prom date had too much to drink and Ryan had found them, pulled the date off her and then had taken her home. She'd been upset, tipsy, and made the horrible mistake of throwing herself at him. That moment had been the one time in her life she'd regretted to this day.

More Books by Debra Clopton

Turner Creek Ranch Series
Treasure Me, Cowboy (Book 1)
Rescue Me, Cowboy (Book 2)
Complete Me, Cowboy (Book 3)
Sweet Talk Me, Cowboy (Book 4)

New Horizon Ranch Series
Her Texas Cowboy (Book 1)
Rafe (Book 2)
Chase (Book 3)
Ty (Book 4)
Dalton (Book 5)
Treb (Book 6)
Maddie's Secret Baby (Book 7)
Austin (Book 8)

Cowboys of Ransom Creek
Her Cowboy Hero (Book 1)
Bride for Hire (Book 2)
Cooper (Book 3)
Shane (Book 4)
Vance (Book 5)
Drake (Book 6)
Brice (Book 7)

Texas Matchmaker Series

Dream With Me, Cowboy (Book 1)

Be My Love, Cowboy (Book 2)

This Heart's Yours, Cowboy (Book 3)

Hold Me, Cowboy (Book 4)

Be Mine, Cowboy (Book 5)

Marry Me, Cowboy (Book 6)

Cherish Me, Cowboy (Book 7)

Surprise Me, Cowboy (Book 8)

Serenade Me, Cowboy (Book 9)

Return To Me, Cowboy (Book 10)

Love Me, Cowboy (Book 11)

Ride With Me, Cowboy (Book 12)

Dance With Me, Cowboy (Book 13)

Windswept Bay Series

From This Moment On (Book 1)

Somewhere With You (Book 2)

With This Kiss (Book 3)

Forever and For Always (Book 4)

Holding Out For Love (Book 5)

With This Ring (Book 6)

With This Promise (Book 7)

With This Pledge (Book 8)

With This Wish (Book 9)

With This Forever (Book 10)

With This Vow (Book 11)

About the Author

Bestselling author Debra Clopton has sold over 2.5 million books. Her book OPERATION: MARRIED BY CHRISTMAS has been optioned for an ABC Family Movie. Debra is known for her contemporary, western romances, Texas cowboys and feisty heroines. Sweet romance and humor are always intertwined to make readers smile. A sixth generation Texan she lives with her husband on a ranch deep in the heart of Texas. She loves being contacted by readers.

Visit Debra's website at www.debraclopton.com

Sign up for Debra's newsletter at
www.debraclopton.com/contest/

Check out her Facebook at
www.facebook.com/debra.clopton.5

Follow her on Twitter at @debraclopton

Contact her at debraclopton@ymail.com

If you enjoyed reading *Forever and For Always* I would appreciate it if you would help others enjoy this book, too.

Recommend it. Please help other readers find this book by recommending it to friends, reader's groups and discussion boards.

Review it. Please tell other readers why you liked this book by reviewing it on the retail site you purchased it from or Goodreads. If you do write a review, please send an email to debraclopton@ymail.com so I can thank you with a personal email. Or visit me at: www.debraclopton.com.